For my father who belives in me.

For my mother who endulges my excentricity.

For my brother who cheers for me.

For my sister who grounds me.

For "Jimmie" James.

For those who have loved me.

For those I have loved.

For Adventure, Intrigue, Mystery, & Romance.

Distant Lands:

Of Sand & the Men Who Died There

An Adventure Novel

By: A.E. Fletcher

Foreword

It was in the waning days of summer when I came upon the person who would present this story to me. I was in London visiting, or rather waiting for, a friend at the time. Simon, my oldest friend in the world, had left our childhood rambling grounds of Southern New Jersey for the hustle and bustle of his ancestral home some eight years prior. He went to make a name and a life for himself, and had inarguably succeeded by the time I finally made my visit. He had married a doctor and become a verger at Suffolk Cathedral, and so there I sat, at the pub just across the way, waiting for the day's final mass to close.

I am a Christian, but as of late had only been a knife-and-fork Christian, arriving mainly for holidays and services that were immediately followed by meals. Only the finest of church lady cuisine. This was why I wasn't at the service. This was why I was in a pub and looking at my second pint's bottom when I noticed the familiar writer seated alone at a back booth.

You are no doubt familiar with his work. Though mostly published under pseudonyms, they are ubiquitous. Some have even been adapted into major motion pictures at this point, and proven to be reliable box office gold. I have no shame in admitting that this particular writer was without a doubt a major influence on my own work, along with Crichton, Doyle, and Bendis.

I was, to put it mildly, star struck. For one due to the aforementioned influence, but also because he had done a fantastic job of hiding all his pertinent personal details over the years. Only a handful of photographs existed. They were as icons; totems to a lonely god of armchair adventure fiction. But, in my traditional near-obsession with my idols, I had seen them many times. Out of respect, I will not betray that job well done, nor offer any pseudonyms as invitation to search.

Never did I once think I would find myself face to face with a hero. If I had, I expect it would not have been a chance meeting in a rather middling London Pub, sadly devoid of the smell of stale beer as part of the Starbuck-ification process that was sweeping the nation's traditional ale houses.

I approached the bar and signaled for two more of the Nut Brown Ale I had been drinking. When the twenty-something bartender placed them in front of me, I beckoned him closer and asked, "Do you know who that is?" pointing at the unassuming form in the back corner.

The bartender just shook his head.

"Sorry. No, mate." And in an instant he was off again.

Now properly armed with the two pints, I made my approach. A calm smile graced my face as my brain screamed in panic, racing to think of something enlightened to say.

I have, of course, committed the entirety of that conversation to memory; however, for brevity's sake, I'll boil it down to the part most pertinent to you: the reader. It was about an hour in when I finally managed to muster up the courage to ask the one question that had been buzzing away in the back of my mind for months. At this moment it was an earsplitting drone. So, I opened my mouth and asked.

"So, what are you working on?"

It had been years since his last project had been published and I had to know. Like a junkie, I needed that one more fix of sweet, vaguely period adventure.

The question caught, but in a manner I didn't expect.

The writer thought for a second, smiled, and reached for an old tattered green cloth bag. Simple in design, it bore a flap closure with two button snaps, and a long, weathered leather strap. He placed the bag on the table, and opened it with some amount of reverence. Slipping out the contents, I could see a very beaten and worn leather book, and a much newer Moleskine. He returned the leather book to the bag and slid the Moleskine across to me.

"This," he responded simply. "Or, I should say I have worked on it. It's done. Near enough of an ending as I can manage. Take it. I've seen your work. Tell the story it tells you. Your reading of it. Suppose when and where you need to, but leave the facts the same. Yours truly excluded."

I reached for it haltingly, but the writer nodded his permission for me to pick it up.

"It's yours," he told me. "I don't need it anymore. The truth is, I've gone off writing. It doesn't hold the same thrill for me these days."

I must have done a poor job of hiding my reaction.

"Read it and you'll understand," he told me.

"What is it? Grave robbers? Nazi treasure? A war story?" I asked in what could have been one breath.

Again, the writer smiled, this time wickedly. "All of the above."

Introduction

Skip was a large man, tall and robust. But in more recent days he allowed age to slope his spine, curving the six-foot man to a more general five-nine. He could, of course, stand up straight when needed, reaching full regimental stature. But, these days, it was rarely needed. Retirement, it would seem, had been the thing to set his body in decline. He would do what he could: lifting the weight he could still manage, doing the cardio his heart would allow, and keeping a clean shave (straight razor was his tool). He wanted to be ready for a day he figured would never come. "Just in case," he told himself often. "Just in case."

On this day he woke up alone in his bed. It was much bigger than he really needed. On the rare occasion when the widow Sophie would come and visit, there was more than room enough for the both of them. He sat up on the bed's edge, stretched, and with something of a wobble, slipped on his slippers and robe before padding his way to the kitchen.

It was early. The hours the elderly keep, tied with a lifetime of military service, added up to one old man doddering around his kitchen before the sun had hardly woken. In those few scattered rays, he set about preparing his day. Rashers and eggs, though his doctor had told him to cut back. He was nearly ninety years old. The time for cutting back had long since passed. They spattered and popped in the cast iron pan, sending up that heavenly aroma. As he had already opened the window, the smell mixed with the mingle of sea spray and countryside scents that were ubiquitous in his little town.

He put the kettle on, as all good English men do, and took down the tin of leaves from the cupboard. No need to measure. He knew just how many spoonfuls to drop in the pot, but first she had to be warmed. The kettle whistled, and he poured just a bit into the pot, swirled it around and dumped it out. Then came the leaves, the rest of the water, and the wait while it steeped. This wasn't an idle wait either. There was important business to be done. Buttering toast and the like. Searching the icebox for the marmalade. (Another item his doctor had said to lay off. But hang the doctor! Were they not English?)

The tea was properly steeped. The eggs, rashers, and

toast were all sorted. Something was missing. Ah! The paper!

Skip shuffled to the door and heard the familiar THUMP as the paper hit the wood. He opened it and saw the rolled bundle on his step and a young man riding away on a bicycle.

"Good morning, Mr. James!" shouted the young man, whose name was Charlie.

"Good morning, Charlie!" shouted Skip in return. "Starting or ending?"

"Starting, Sir."

Skip smiled. "Ah, you'll have to be up earlier tomorrow."

He crouched down with more ease than one might expect having seen him, and scooped up the paper before tucking it into his robe pocket.

The sun was fully awake now, and as Skip looked down, he saw the little town following suit. The early morning joggers were out in force. Young mothers pushed their prams alongside one another, sharing the latest gossip of the other young mothers in town. Shop keepers were beginning to lay out their A-frame signs with the latest in deals and specials written in calligraphic chalk lettering, and surrounded with playful sketch work.

Charlie had been right. It was, Skip decided, a good morning. In the next moment, it suddenly occurred to him that his eggs were rapidly cooling, and he hurried back to them.

Skip's home, a two-story free stander on the hill overlooking the village, wasn't showy. It wasn't by any stretch modest but what it held, it held with dignity. Traditional white brick and a brown clay tile roof, it was hemmed in on the sides by slopping green hills, and stood at the end of a long road that weaved down into the little town.

It was, however, the inside that would impress, were you to visit. It was decorated top to bottom with the relics of past adventures and forgotten glories. That was a truth that none would tell: that when you had lived as long and seen as much as Skip and his mates had, you could easily forget any event that would have made another man's life. The mundanity of the extraordinary.

The living room was adorned with masks, framed bits of parchment signed by some great nineteenth century explorer, and photographs. He and his mates standing with long lost tribes, or knee deep in some forgotten treasure. Some of that treasure was still in the attic, as you may have guessed. However, it was a topic of much gossip in the little town of

whether it actually existed, if it ever existed, or how much of it might be left. Occasionally, the teens would dare one of their kind to scale the hill, and attempt to break in during the night to see. But, invariably, they'd see Skip cleaning one of his guns, or sharpening one of the blades he had collected. Be it scimitar or Springfield, the image was equally disturbing for his habit of doing it without the aid of light. Old or not, a military man is a military man.

You may be happy to know that the eggs weren't too cold when he had got to them, and the tea was just how he liked it, strong and just below scalding. He pulled a small flask from the pocket of his robe, added a couple drops of its contents to the tea, sipped it, and munched one of the rashers while unfurling the paper, and returning the flask to its place.

The news was much as it ever was. Strife in the halls of Parliament, anger on the streets, and gossip about celebrities he had long since given up on keeping track of. He turned the page and there found a little note, a small scrap of torn white paper about four inches across, with a simple message written in blue fountain pen:

THEY ARE COMING FOR YOU

And then, below that:

TWO DAYS

Skip looked at it for a moment, turned it over in his

hands, and put it back down before turning to the next page. He knew who it was from. He could recognize that handwriting as sure as his own. He knew who the "THEY" referred to as well from recent correspondence.

When he was done with his breakfast, and thoroughly finished with the paper, Skip stood and went up to his bedroom. He took a suit from his closet and grabbed a waistcoat, shirt, shoes, suspenders, and a bow tie to match. Once he was dressed he headed into the study where the lion's share of his gun collection stood on lighted oak shelves, always clean, always ready for action. He gazed over them, screwing up his face in thought.

It was only a few moments later that Skip stepped out his front door, cane in hand, and started his walk down the hill. He could hear the gulls and the sea. Those fishing boats that were going out for the day had long since gone, but the bay still housed a few.

As he walked, he checked his pocket watch. *Still a bit early to go round the pub*, he thought. But, he could use a walk for the exercise. He considered this as he approached the intersection. It was, however, a lovely time to call on the widow Sophie.

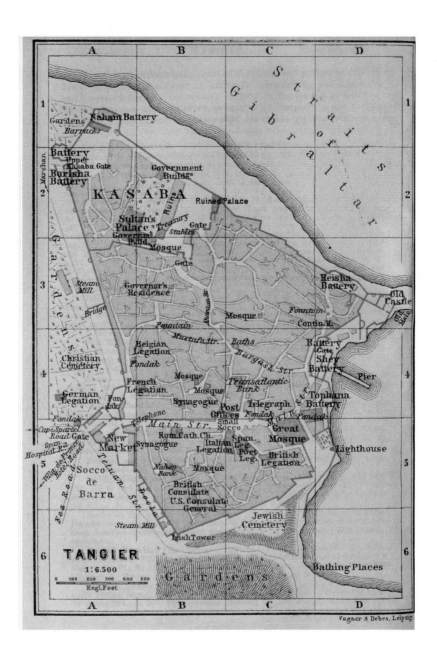

TANGIER

1 : 6.500

0   100   200   300   400   500
Engl.Feet

Vagner & Debes, Leipzig

14

Chapter 1

Ridley had become what he hated. After a truly
amazing night, he had awoken alone in bed. Or rather he
thought he was alone. He had forgotten she was there. That was
not a brag. It was more of a symptom of the late, hash-filled
nights that, at the time, made up more of his weeks than not.
It was early. Ungodly so. Why was he awake? The sun wasn't
even up. Was it morning? Did it even count as morning?

With a not-too-inconsiderable amount of effort, he
rolled over just in time to catch her in the midst of slipping her
pants up over her long muscular legs. His first thought was that
the action, to his mind, seemed somehow a quantifiable wrong.
He told her as much. She cracked the same smile she had
given him many times the night before. All teeth with a bit of
gum, a little crooked, and very, very aware of his level of, and
penchant for, rye humor.

"Are you getting up?" she asked.

"Eventually. I suppose," he said, going up onto one elbow and striking the "Burt Reynolds" pose. "Why in God's name are you?"

She grabbed a random piece of string from the dresser and tied her hair up into a utilitarian ponytail.

"Because, my rogue adventurer, some of us have bills to pay."

"I have bills," he said in something very akin to a pout. Akin to a pout but not a real pout. Adults do not pout.

"Yes, but yours seem to be, by all appearances, on autopilot these days," she said, having moved on to lacing her heavy leather boots. They were old, but cared for. Not in the sense of having not been used, but rather having been used within a breath of their limit, then serviced, repaired, and taken out into the field again. The feet within them trusted none other.

She wasn't wrong, of course. Ridley couldn't for the life of him remember the last time he had personally paid a bill. He knew that no one was after him for rent at that very moment and assumed they would be, were that a thing to be concerned about. His manager, Dona Feldman, was probably taking care of that stuff. Yeah. That sounded about right. Good on, Donna.

The now fully-clothed woman standing in his apartment and questioning his bill paying processes was Carly. Carly was a photographer. A photographer who came to Tangier to take a number of photos for another spread in that travel magazine. You know the one. That old American standard of institutional culture found in the dentists' offices and supermarket checkout racks around the globe. The wonders of the world condensed to a collection of so many pages and photographs written and taken by some of the last true adventurers, neatly framed in yellow; boxed in by the latest celebrity gossip trash and the top thirty-seven absolute musts for the modern new bride.

Hers would be another piece on Paul Bowles and the Beat Generation. Somehow, in the hundreds of years that Tangier had stood, it would seem to the general magazine-reading public that those twenty years were the only points of interest here on offer to the outside man. Those covetous dreams of hash and revolutionary human thought.

"It sells," she said matter-of-factly. Truth be told, Ridley couldn't argue with her. It was similarly romanticized armchair adventure that had set him out on his own journey so very long ago.

After one more final go through of her gear, from the floor, Carly flipped up her ponytail in a swift movement and held it over her shoulder. She looked up and smiled at him before crawling to the bed's edge, slipping her hands into his shaggy beard, and planting an impassioned kiss on his stupidly lucky lips. He accepted and returned it.

"I had fun," she said.

"Me, too," he smirked.

"Will I see you tonight?"

Ridley shrugged. "You know where to find me."

"I might find your creature-of-habitness off-putting if you weren't so damn cute."

"Well then, I will do my absolute best to keep it up."

"And humble to boot."

She left and he lay there alone for a long while, half covered by a white linen sheet, dipping in and out of consciousness.

The Mu'adhan began their morning call to prayer, a gust of wind carrying the atonal chorus in through the windows that he had somehow never once closed since moving in. The curtains billowed as if conducting that chorus.

"At some point," he mused to himself, "I should probably learn what the hell they are saying."

As with most of the languages he spoke, Ridley knew

just enough Arabic to get through a day without needing to resort to clumsy, often accidentally phallic, hand gestures. However, it was also enough to regularly get him knee deep into a conversation and not know how to get himself back out. More than once he had found himself endeavoring to commit the simple act of small talk, and instead ending up awash in words far outside the safe and lovely confines of his [Insert language here] to English paperback books. The same books would protrude limply from his back pocket in these moments. Unreached for. Unnoticed. Unable to help even if he had.

Maybe that was why he had settled in Tangier. The Amsterdam of North Africa, as it had been called by a television chef, and assumedly others. The old talk was that at one point expatriates had eventually outnumbered the natives in the city center. But, as the realization that being an artist in search of the romantic life was not enough to pay the bills began to finally hit that tragically hip generation, the numbers began to drop. They lowered but never dwindled. Here he had found more than a few like minds. His "Tribe" as his mother had called them. Those who had hit the road long ago, in search of something so very "other." On that, Tangier would deliver in spades.

Ridley rolled out of the bed and sat on its edge, head in hands, for a moment just long enough so that the room could stop its nauseating warble. When the all too familiar feeling a friend had once termed a "high over" finally eased up just enough, he staggered to a crumpled pair of khakis that sat in a ball on the floor. They had landed there in last night's frenzied need to get them off, and any other scrap of clothing along with them. At the very least, he was able to find them this time. That was a small blessing. For how sparsely decorated his home was, he had lost quite a bit of clothing in these evening activities. Socks, shoes...he was fairly certain a few bras were probably concealed somewhere, long since abandoned by their equally forgotten wearers.

Finding a white button-down that had not yet been sweat-stained through, he threw it on along with a pair of leather sandals and his satchel, and set off to start another day in paradise.

The revolving door that had become his bedroom was a point of wounded pride for Ridley. He had never meant to become that man. He hated the very notion of being that man. The serial lothario was an image that felt ill-suited to him in his mind, if not in life. But, the more he had traveled, the more it seemed to grow on him. Settling here had not, in any way, helped. As the adventure and romance seekers came in their droves, he became something of a curiosity to them. To them, he was equal parts a familiar taste of home and something exotic and mysterious. The elusive expat.

-

How the hell had he gotten here? He was one of the adventure seekers himself once. A cubical dweller with an imagination bigger than the job he had sat in for just a little too long. He wrote a book, expecting nothing to come of it. Something did. Reviewers would say he had tapped into something, and the people, bless 'em, wanted more. The seduction of a life without ties took hold, and Ridley spent the next few years making the rounds.

Amsterdam, Yangon, Cuzco. Anywhere he could write, he wrote, collecting stories and continuing the adventures of "Rex Morgan: Rogue Adventurer." Cheesy, yes. We can all agree. But, someone was buying it and the residuals kept him moving, even between advances.

In the end, that was what he had needed more than anything else. He just had to keep moving. In the deepest corners of his mind, he believed if he moved fast enough the feelings could not catch him. But, it was his penchant for collecting stories that brought him to Morocco. And, it was the chance meeting he had with an old man by the name of

Nicolas Burns that kept him here long enough to start the roots growing.

—

Ridley had met Nick at the now infamous Café Baba, a diverse little hang out that will probably outlive every printed copy of this book. Clientele ranging from foreign students (in t-shirts and jeans) to old men (in tweed and knit ties), all of which much higher than most of you have or ever will be, discussing the intricacies of global politics with the fervor of freshman political science majors, but with the life experience of those who had actually seen the globe.

Ridley was still new at the time. He had only been in town for a couple of days at that point and was staying in a hostel just outside of the Medina. One of those visually loud, modern design nightmares that lives and dies purely on the allure of 20-something world travel. Word around the hostel's outdoor bar was that Café Baba was the place to go if you wanted really "authentic Tangier." Though, the word "authentic" had lost all meaning in the past few years. With that ringing endorsement from the intensely baked Germans standing waist deep in the pool, he set off.

The café's seafoam green walls bore photographs of the many who had passed through their arched doorways. Artists and Generals alike had sat and shared the pipe in those halls. Those moments were frozen in black and white, hung about in a mildly haphazard fashion, and occasionally scrutinized by their intoxicated forbearers, each of which genuinely believing they were the first to notice said photographs. All of them conjecturing about their topics.

Obviously, the memory of which of them, Ridley or Nick, had first struck up the conversation is lost to the ages and a purple haze. But Ridley could tell near instantly that Nick was a rare find in this life. They talked about history. Rather, Ridley talked about history. The old man had actually lived it. Not just in the sense that any elderly person could say they had "lived history." Sure, by your simple existence you have survived enough world events to safely make that claim. But, Nick was among those rare few who had actively taken part in the making of that history. He would tell stories about his time on the North African front, going toe to toe with Rommel's forces, in adventures that could have very easily been unaired episodes of Rat Patrol. His stories had people in them with names like Skip and Ponsley.

When the two of them had finally staggered out of Café Baba, Nick deftly guided his new charge to the little Spanish

Tortilla place across the street. They sat on the steps munching the potato and egg concoction with little to no concern for appearances or decorum while the old man continued, "And Skip…you know Skip. He could drive those dunes like they were the Queen's roads. Effortless. And you need that when you're dodging Jerry's birds."

He'd gesture with his hands, showing how the old warplanes would bear down on them. "They'd come down and, DAKKA DAKKA DAKKA! Ponsley and I with nothing but our pea shooters, and Skip would just weave. Serpentine. Calm as a Sunday."

From then on Ridley had been back every night. It happed to work out that Nick, too, was a creature of habit. With his permission Ridley began to take notes of his stories, and eventually started recording them. The old man's voice, he believed, was such a part of it. That trembling scraggle born of a lifetime of hookah smoke. Each word sounded all the more powerful for having made it out through the gauntlet. Refugees of impending stage four throat cancer.

Eventually, as one might expect, Nick had made it home from the war, returning to his little village in the north of England. But, the war had changed him, and not just in the way it changes a man to take a life, or several. Nick now bore the curse of a man who had seen the world beyond his country home's low stone walls and grassy hills. He had seen the world and something deep in his belly now burned for him to be in it and of it.

How far he had come from that little village.

-

Ridley made his way through the streets of the Medina as he did every day. At this point he could probably have navigated them blindfolded were it not for the street merchants whose "shops" seemed to occupy a different square of ground from one day to the next. He found one that sold fruit and bought himself an apple. Munching it, he was thankful for the little bit of highness that carried over from last night, allowing him to really taste that apple in all its juicy glory. It was the little things.

He arrived at the little café where he and Nick had eventually moved their daily extended conversations. A little more out of the way. A little more private. Between the two of them, they probably kept the place open as it was quite rare to see anyone else, aside from the occasional lost tourist, stop in. He sat and without hesitation Khalid, the proprietor, came out and poured him a small cup of coffee.

"Thank you, Khalid. Good morning."

Khalid nodded and smiled. "Very good."

He waited with an expectant grin while Ridley scanned through his hazy brain and suddenly it dawned on him.

"She had it?!"

"Yes. Yes. A boy! Praise Allah."

Ridley reached out and patted him on the back. "Congratulations!"

"Thank you. Thank you."

"And Safae?"

"They are both very well."

"I'm glad. That's amazing!"

Khalid smiled and went back in and started on breakfast. Ordering was not the kind of thing one did there. You came in and Khalid cooked. That was the extent of the agreement. No negotiations. No substitutions. If you had a food allergy, you took your business elsewhere. Khalid, even before he became a father, had no time for your anaphylaxis. The fact that the two men had been coming here every day for four months and were neither tired of his choices nor disappointed in a single instance should stand as a testament to the chef's command of his medium.

Ridley sipped his coffee for a bit before digging through his bag for a voice recorder, a sketch book, and some pencils. Nick would assumedly be along shortly. Setting a specific appointment with him had proven to be ultimately pointless. The old man kept them like a wizard. Never early. Never late. Arriving exactly when he intended to. In all fairness, it did lend something to his mystique.

When Nicolas Burns finally showed, Khalid was just setting down their breakfast plates. Eggs with olives, fresh fruit, and lots of flat bread and butter. Nick rounded the corner looking as though he had stepped out of the Oxford English Dictionary definition of the word "expatriate." He wore an old suit with a scarf languidly tossed over his shoulder, round sunglasses, and a Muslim taqiyah crowning his head. He moved with a dance-like step and wielded a cane that was intended more for show than ever being truly necessary.

Taking his seat, he paid greetings and compliments to Khalid.

"We'll have to remember to tip large today," Ridley told him. "Khalid here is a father now."

Again they went through the series of obligatory congratulations and well wishes before Khalid left them to their very important business of café talk, happily busying himself with something or other inside the restaurant.

"And what about you?" the old man asked pointedly.

"What about me?"

He eyed the young man with the look of someone who already knew what they wanted, but wanted to hear it out loud.

"That girl. The photographer. What was her name? Kaity?"

"Carly," Ridley replied, knowing full well that he knew exactly what her name was.

"Ah. Yes. Darling girl. You two seemed to hit it off quite nicely." He let the penny hang in the air, waiting for the rest of the story's details to be filled in and fleshed out.

Ridley just leaned back and smiled. "Really?"

The sat in silence for a moment before the laughter they were both holding back threatened to burst them at the seams.

"You can't blame an old man for attempting to live vicariously through his younger avatar in this world."

"A damn dirty old man."

"Damn guilty as charged." He held up his wrists. "Lock

me up." They laughed together. It was pure and unambiguous.

This had become a somewhat regular way of starting their days. As night would close in, the secluded street would inevitably find itself host to a few of the aforementioned tourists who had made one or two wrong turns. Ridley would always offer his assistance to direct them back to where they had come from; however, the lady travelers would occasionally stay, intrigued by he and the old man's relationship. As mentioned earlier, they had become curiosities. Living evidence and reinforcement of the city's enduring artistic image.

After a certain hour, Nick would excuse himself, complaining about the weariness of old age, and the girls would ask Ridley how to find this little place they had heard of. More often than not, that little place was Café Baba. In the morning Nick would ask after them, trying and failing to be sly about it. It was the nature of things.

"What do you want me to say? Did we sleep together? Yes. Yes, Nick. The young lady and I had our ways with one another. It was passionate. Breathless. An erotic masterpiece worthy of D.H. Lawrence."

Nick grumbled in return. "Petulant and esoteric."

"To the last," Ridley replied with a smile.

Nick took out a pipe. The same pipe Ridley had seen

him smoke many times, though he knew he owned others. "This one's grown to fit my hand," the old man would tell him. Though, he began to suspect it was the reverse. Nick proceeded to pull little pinches of tobacco from the packet concealed in his jacket pocket.

"You know," he began, striking a match, "I've told you a good number of stories."

"Some of them repeatedly."

"And, all I ask is the occasional conversational dalliance." He puffed away, eyebrow arched and thumb in his waistcoat pocket.

Ridley remained stone-faced. "Are you ready to start?"

A sinister grin crept to the old man's lips, and he burst out laughing. "Oh. I see."

"See what?"

"You like this one. You, the great American lover, have found yourself smitten. Struck down by Cupid's sure aim."

"Oh, God. You're not going to drop this, are you?"

He was not wrong. When Carly first came ambling down the street outside Khalid's she had seemed like any of the others, but once they had gotten down to talking, Ridley immediately knew better. She was different. Funny, well-read, and quick. "The Old Man and his Boswell" she had called them.

-

"So, this is what you two do?" she had asked him that first night, after Nick had excused himself. "Drink coffee and tell war stories?"

"At some point Khalid switches us from coffee to tea. Not really sure when that happens, but he does."

"Not a bad way to live, I suppose."

"There are definitely worse ways to make a living."

They wandered for a bit. The shops were closing down but he successfully managed to get them a Majoon for the night. A large, fist sized, sphere made of a mixture of nuts, fruit, chocolate, honey, and a large amount of kief, it was guaranteed to do what they needed it to do.

"I don't make a habit of doing drugs with strangers," she told him.

"Yeah. That's probably a good policy to keep. As a rule I personally do not do anything you have to shoot, snort, or

31

take as a pill."

She considered this for a moment. "Clean and green? I can get behind that."

They found themselves a nice little spot overlooking the ports and Ridley handed her the Majoon.

"Such a gentleman," she said, raising it to her mouth and breathing in its strong smell through her nose.

"I was raised right."

"How much do I take?" she asked.

"I figured we'd split it. Get a little transcendental." He smiled.

They did and decided to just sit for a bit while they waited for the time bomb of highness to kick in.

She told him about her family. Two brothers, one of which had died in a motorcycle accident and the other who was a tax accountant in one of those states whose main export was cows and the components of cows. Her mom was a teacher and her dad had been a war correspondent. He was one of the lucky. Eventually made it home and started teaching college classes in journalism and about ethics in the fog of war. He wanted a family more than the thrill life. But, his first love lived on in her. He taught her how to shoot, bought her first camera, and introduced her to some friends of his who had never left the game. She was now a photo journalist in her own right, and one of some repute.

"What about you? Did you choose the thrill life over family?" Ridley asked her before he realized how loaded of a question it sounded.

She thought about it for a moment.

"I'm not sure yet. I mean, there's always that part of you that thinks, 'Yeah. That would be nice.' But, how do you give up all this?" She gestured broadly at the night sky and city lights. "We are about to be high out of our minds in Morocco! How ridiculous is that? No matter how long I do this work, I never want to stop being amazed by things like that."

Ridley smiled. He understood what she meant. He, of course, also had a family back home. He would stop in every once in a while to the cheers of progressively taller nieces and nephews. His sister chiding him when the stories he told of the wild life of a global citizen headed a bit too far in the direction of blue. At no point had he ever really stopped thinking about how it would feel to be a parent. To raise a little him. But, she was right. How could anyone give up all this?

The world started to go wavy as the majoon broke down in their stomachs.

33

"What do you say? Wanna get out of here?" he asked her in the smoothest voice he could manage.

"Go home with the rogue adventurer? I don't know. Should I?"

"Are you asking me? Because…."

"Fair enough," she laughed. "Lay on, MacDuff."

They got back to his place after making several wrong turns and, with increasingly inaccurate hand movements, began to remove one another's clothes.

"Wait," she said. "We need music."

He wobbled in place for a moment as his brain attempted to associate her words with any known meaning before realizing that what she had said was the greatest idea of all time.

"You are an angel, queen, goddess, and a damned genius."

With much effort he was able to find where he had put his record player (six months ago) and his copy of Revolver. He dropped the needle on Tomorrow Never Knows and took a running dive into the bed.

The room was a blurry swirl of color and sound. A razor sharp dullness. Like an art deco building with the corners sanded to curves. That was it. Being high was like Art Nouveau. All organic forms and thoughts in dazzling clarity. But you weren't allowed to keep them. Just look. Never touch. And never ever put to use.

"Perfect," she purred as he slid his hand to the small of her back.

The rest was lost in the haze.

—

Nick spooned up the last of his couscous and popped it into his mouth. It was getting late. The sun had already disappeared beyond the rooftops and Khalid came out to clear their late afternoon snack plates.

"Have I told you about the time I bought a treasure map from a street urchin in Calcutta?"

He had. Enough times that Khalid shifted Ridley a knowing glance before walking off.

"No. Go ahead."

"Well, it was 1956. I was just arriving in town and this little bastard ran up and tried to knick my wallet. I had not

35

learned yet how to hide it. Special pocket, stitched to the inside trim of your trousers. Just around here. I had a tailor do up all my trousers that way. A lovely man in Marrakech. Anyway, I caught the little beggar by the wrist and nearly throttled him. But, he was all skin and bone. I think I almost broke his arm when I grabbed him, he was so thin.

"He says to me 'Please, please, Mister. I'm hungry.' In Hindi of course, but I had just come from Delhi so I was picking it up here and there. He makes me a deal. Says he has this map and he will sell it to me for thirty rupees. I figure, why the bloody hell not? I feed the kid and he gives me the map. Even if it's a fake, I've got a story.

"So I buy the map off him and he goes scampering off. Turns out it leads to a place the locals call 'The Forbidden Mansion.' My interest, needless to say, was piqued. So, I go out to this mansion. It is far out there, deep in the dark of the jungle. All overgrown. Covered in a net of the…the…the vines. Mind you. I had just got to town. I had not even bathed. I had just bought a few samosas for the road and went out into the jungle like a damn fool. So, now here I am, trying to squeeze between these damn vines because it hadn't crossed my mind to bring a bloody machete. I get inside and–"

"What are you boys up to?" Carly interrupted with a smile.

She was wearing the same clothes she had left him in, but Ridley was still struck by the sight of her. Her sweat-through tank top, dirty khakis, and camera hanging loose at her side made her beautiful–adventure neatly encapsulated in a single woman.

Nick gave him a knowing glance before turning to her.

"Just regaling my Boswell with a few tales of my daring do."

"Were there Nazis in this one?"

"Ah! I shan't spoil the mystery," the old man said.

Ridley hit stop on his recorder. "Forbidden treasures in the jungles of India."

Nick shook his head. "No sense of showmanship, this one. You'll need to learn theatricality, my boy!"

"I would like to hear that one sometime," said Carly.

Nick stood and stretched like an old, fat cat in the afternoon sun. "Perhaps another time, my dear. Old bones are not meant for nights as late as these."

"Okay, Nick. Have a good night," Ridley stood and they hugged. "Take care."

"You too," he whispered before pulling back and giving

a tactless wink.

That dirty old man.

Carly and Ridley watched as Nick wandered off down the lane, half expecting his dance-like stride to culminate in a swing around a lamp post that never came.

"Is he going to be okay?" she asked.

Ridley laughed. "That man will outlive all of us."

He had, of course, been expecting her and had gone ahead and ordered them dinner to go.

"God you're an ass," Carly said, flashing a wry grin at the sight of the pre-packaged meal as Khalid set it down in front of them.

-

They immediately went back to his place. The new father had prepared them lamb tagine with bread and mint tea, and they sat on the floor, eating it with their hands. Electric Ladyland was on the turn table and they passed the mouthpiece of his hookah back and forth.

"Get any good shots today?"

"A few."

She crawled across the floor to her camera bag before returning and scooting up alongside him.

"Check this one out."

She turned the camera on and quickly scrolled through several gorgeous images of the market before settling on one and handing him the camera. It was a spice shop. The neatly ordered and giant mounds of spice balanced by the little old woman in traditional garb selling them. The colors were rich and vibrant. Almost painful in their vividness. Beautiful.

"This is really…. Wow. I mean…really."

"It's okay," she shrugged. "It's my favorite of the day, but there are a few others the magazine will probably buy."

She took a deep pull on the hookah and handed it back to him. "What about you? Does Rex Morgan have a new adventure calling his name yet?"

"Maybe," he blew out a dragon-like plume of smoke before handing the mouth piece back to her. "He told me one earlier in the day about a trip to Rio with a team who were sent looking for Percy Fawcett. Could be something workable there."

"I'm just going to smile, nod, and pretend I know who

39

that is."

"How do you not?" He asked her with genuine incredulity. "You work for–"

"I just shoot the pictures," she cut in. "There is a whole other team putting the words and history to them."

Ridley took a second to square that thought in his mind before deciding it didn't mean his life was a lie, and moving on.

"Okay. Fawcett was an old British Colonel and member of the Royal Geographical Society. He was part of this major effort they were doing to map the world. His specialty was South America. The Amazon. He would load up with supplies and crew, head out into the jungle, and six months later stumble back out filthy, emaciated, and with a giant bag full of maps hanging off him by a leather strap. This guy befriended tribes that had never seen the outside world before. He supposedly shot an anaconda on one of his trips. We're talking a big damn hero adventurer."

"On some Indiana Jones shit. Got it."

He leaned in and kissed her for that.

"Thank you. Right. Ok. But where it gets interesting is that he believed the Vikings had crossed the Atlantic and settled in what would eventually become Brazil, before anyone else had. He was obsessed with the idea. It had to be him to prove it, too. So, the race was on. Of course, World War One had to go and get in the way."

"Those pesky global conflicts."

So, the British army calls him back. He's deployed! All officers are needed. Supposedly, he was so nuts by the end of it he was using a Ouija board to decide where to send artillery strikes."

"That seems stable."

"By the time he comes back, he is disgraced. Nobody wants to fund him, travel with him. I mean no one. Like people used to line up to go on a Fawcett expedition. It was a status symbol in the adventure community. But now, the only people he can get to go with him are his oldest son and his son's best friend. So, the three of them wander off into the jungle and are never seen again."

"Wow."

"Yeah, wow. And over six hundred people have gone missing looking for them. Nick just happened to be one of the ones that made it back. Got a bad infection and had to be carried out of the jungle on a stretcher."

"You should probably leave that part out."

"Meh. I could probably just have Rex be the one carrying him."

"That Rex. He is quite the hero."

"He does what he can." Ridley leaned in and kissed her again. Passionately this time.

"Somehow I knew you were going to make me listen to that whole story before you did that."

"Call it dramatic timing."

"I'll just call you an ass and save time."

"And Nick said I had no sense of showmanship."

She joked, but he knew she had the same thirst for knowledge, for adventure, as he did. No one would choose this life if they didn't. He silently damned Nick for being so right. He actually liked her.

They talked a bit more, finishing dinner and switching the hookah from tobacco to hash. He turned down the lights and the room was lit only by the little stained glass lanterns that peppered the ceiling. The wind gently pushed them about as the two of them lay on their backs, watching the light dance and the kaleidoscopic patterns they formed shift.

He rolled over and kissed her. It was not the kind of kiss he would have given any of the many others who had traipsed through his one-man harem. This was a kiss of care. A kiss of tender weariness. Of unguarded loneliness. A kiss that could not stay just a kiss. They clawed at one another, gasping for breath and whispering uninhibited confessions to one another.

"Don't go back to the states," he told her. "I need you here."

"I love you." She blurted it out and seemed to regret it the moment she said it.

Suddenly she was bashful. He pulled back and looked her in the eyes. Those gorgeous green eyes. She was somehow more beautiful in this moment than she had ever been. Her wavy, black hair tossed about and cascading across the pillows. How could she love him? So fast. So soon. But, he knew what she meant. He knew deep in his heart of hearts that she was the woman he had been looking for all this time without knowing he was looking at all. Damn it.

"I love you, too."

Chapter 2

The man who called himself Nicolas Burns walked home on the winding roads of the Medina. Home. It was a quaint concept to him even now. Home was where the heart was, he had oft heard said. But, his life was long and he had lost track of just where that might have been. These days, the place he called home was a little two-bedroom that overlooked the city and the sea. His heart, or what was left of it, felt at peace here. A privilege he thought he may never have known.

He arrived at the old, ornately carved Cedar door, and fumbled for the bulky ring of keys in his pocket. The plurality of those "keys" neatly straddled that line of affect and sentimentality. In truth, he only needed the one. But, every other key on that ring had at some point been a key to his home. All the homes he had lived in, with all the hearts he had forgotten, and even those he still tried in vain to forget.

Unlocking the door, he entered, and removed his scarf, hat, and jacket before moving onto the important work of recovering the bottle of Scotch he had stowed under the sideboard. Alcohol was illegal in the Medina, and though he doubted a raid, he couldn't deny that there was still a subconscious thrill to a secretly hidden bottle. Once upon a time he had hidden jewels. Now he hid the means of reminiscence.

He crouched down and reached under the sidebar, all the way to the back and up. A slight opening had only just fit the bottle, and he grabbed it. There was a soft rumble and a thud. Nick looked down to see that something else had fallen out of the hole. It was a small canvas sack, caked thickly with dust, and bearing the emblem of Her Majesty's Eighth Army. He picked it up and stood, cracking his back as he went.

Nick poured himself three thick fingers of the peaty contraband, and ambled through the organized chaos that was his living room before settling in his favorite high backed chair and seeing to the canvas-wrapped parcel. He turned it over in his trembling hands. Painfully, he knew what it would be before he opened it, and just why he had hidden it in the first place. He opened the sack.

Inside was a worn, old leather book, stuffed with newspaper clippings, paper scraps, and photographs. Once he had pulled the book out, a glint caught his eye. Reaching back in, he found its source: a heavy gold ring, fitted with a large red rock about the size of a pistachio. Of all he had seen and all he had done, these two objects brought more hell and ruin into his life than any others.

The book's worn leather cover bore almost no distiguishing marks beyond the image of a black eagle stamped into its front. Even that showed age. It's terrible cargo scratched free from its talons by age. Nick had seen that eagle more times and, in more places than he ever cared to remember. Borne up proudly by the men he knew as enemies.

He opened the book, and ignored the words scribbled on the inside cover. Even now they were committed to his memory. Instead he turned to the photograph that lay face down opposite them. Written on the back in a light script was:

BURNS, SKIP, PONSLEY 1953

He slowly turned it over to reveal the young faces of him and his friends. Friends. Or rather, those who had once been considered friends. Life had its complicated ways. He spent the next hour or so turning through the familiar pages. He hadn't seen them in years, but knew them each in detail. As he felt the weary hand of sleep descending over his eyes, Nick closed the book and placed it on his lap.

47

He looked at the ring. It glinted in the low light. The blood red stone and the buttery gold seemed a stock still blaze. A thought occurred to him, and he opened the drawer in his side table, fishing around for paper, pen, and envelope. He wrote a letter, addressed it to Ridley, then sealed it and the ring in the envelope before tucking it between his leg and the arm of the chair.

When he was done, he glanced in the direction of his bedroom. He really should go to bed, he thought. But the chair was very comfortable. Overstuffed and broken in so that the cushioning would wrap around him. *Just a nip*, he thought. Then he would go to bed. Rest his eyes, then….

-

They woke up intertwined, only stirred by the Mu'adhan reciting the morning call to prayer.

"Do you know what they're saying?" Carly asked.

"Not a clue," said Ridley.

"They'll start with the Takbir, proclaiming 'God is great.' Then they'll say the Shahada. 'There is no god but God, Muhammad is the messenger of God.'"

He looked at her, not even remotely surprised. Of course she knew.

"Good morning."

"Good morning."

They kissed, and after an extended session of morning lovemaking, went about their preparations for the day much as they had the day before. The only real differences being a few more lingering glances, and several more lingering kisses.

When she finally went off, it was in search of some images more salable than the previous day's work. They promised to meet up at Khalid's again that night. Ridley slipped out a bottle of whiskey and poured himself a glass, feeling as though he had earned it. To live this life and find the love of a good woman was a feat in itself. How they would make it work, he had nothing even bordering on an idea. But, that was another day's problem. Today he was young, in love, and looking out over a city rich with Byronic romance.

-

Ridley set off for Khalid's with his gear in hand and mused, thankfully, that his daily work required remarkably less equipment than Carly's. She tried to carry as many lenses and cameras as she could without wearing the invisible "Rob Me, I Am American" sign. He respected her work, of course, but not the hassle. Granted, at some point he would eventually need to turn to the task of converting Nick's stories into actual narrative fiction, but that was yet another of tomorrow's problems.

He decided to try a different route this day, looping around by the leather tanners, and stepping into the atmosphere of warm wet air that hung over their square like a curtain. The men walked with deft skill along the narrow walls of their massive stone tanks, stirring and churning the hot boiled leather. The tanks were in clusters of roughly twenty, and several of these clusters packed the three-square-block area. Ridley wove between them, on through the leather market and across to Khalid's.

It was rare that he was bothered, even as a foreigner. A man had tried to rob him once when he first moved to town. Less robbery, more pick pocketry, but Ridley's policy of reinforcing his bags' zippers with small metal hooks, made them just enoying enough that most would be pickpockets moved on without their prize. These days, it seemed the tone of his skin, kink of his hair, and the thick scrub of beard he hadn't cut, beyond a trim, in over a year, marked him as, if not a native, a foreigner who "got it."

Ridley's coffee was poured with the bleary eyes and shaking hands of a new father.

"Not much sleep?"

"No. The crying." Khalid had no stamina for small talk. Ridley thought it better not to press him on it, and the poor proprietor took that as a mercy. In all honesty he was just thankful to still be getting breakfast at all. The thought never occurred to him that one day Khalid might not be there, and he and Nick would be forced to move their day's work to another establishment. Perish the thought. Ridley instead sipped his coffee and glanced about at the narrow street he had come to spend his every day on. There was so much about it he had somehow never noticed.

So rapt by Nick's stories, he had not paid any mind to the little things, like the crack in the wall opposite him extending from ground to roof. It was neither new nor important, but in that moment he found it infinitely fascinating. The whole street had a new feel about it, as if someone had changed the filter on the camera of his perception.

Today's a good day, Ridley thought.

Khalid brought out two plates of soft cheese wrapped in palm leaves and a large stack of flat bread, and disappeared back into the restaurant without a word. The words "poor bastard" waltzed though Ridley's mind as he set about the task of methodically dividing up his cheese and pairing it with the still warm, pillowy flat bread. Absolutely beyond delicious.

He took out his digital voice recorder, sketch book, and pencils, and continued to eat, vaguely wondering how late Nick would be. Not late. Never late. Never early. Would he tell him about Carly? He hadn't decided yet. The thought of his smug expression upon hearing of their loving declarations was almost too much.

"You can't live this life in tandem," the old man had told him once in an uncharacteristically vulnerable moment. "Love breeds contentment and contentment breeds settling down. No matter how long you live, do not ever settle down."

Ridley had to admit, he had taken those words a little closer to heart than he knew he should have. Nick was basically reinforcing what he had already tricked himself into believing. But, it was a haunting moment when it dawned on him that he was Nick's only friend. The old man had led the life he himself claimed so much to want, but there was not a single other soul to ask after him during their long uninterrupted cafe days. Ridley may not have known what he wanted, but he knew it was something more than what he had.

The day rolled on and Ridley continued to wait.

Shadows shifted and retreated as the sun's rays began to beat them back and descend into the alley. He filled the time, listening to Khalid tell all about his night of happy delirium and sleeplessness, and roughly sketching Rex Morgan heroically dragging a wounded ally from the jungle. He checked his watch–a cheap pocket deal he had picked up from a street vendor for five American dollars.

Nick had never been this late. Concern for the old man started to creep into Ridley's mind, but he dismissed it just as quickly. The tough old bird was probably off somewhere buying another trinket of curious origin to add to the inarguably impressive collection he had amassed.

A few more hours passed and the sun stood high above, triumphant in its short skirmish with the morning shadows. Khalid came and opened the umbrella, as per usual, to shield them– him–from the direct baking heat. Where the hell was Nick? He would have called him, but the old luddite refused to carry a cell phone, smart or otherwise. "I only want to be reached by those near enough to do so with their own two hands," he would say whenever Ridley brought up the idea.

-

Carly swung by just as the sun began to retreat again, giving way to its old enemy and casting the whole world into vivid shades of orange and purple.

"Did Nick take off already?"

"He never showed up," Ridley said, sipping his tea with a furrowed brow.

Her face mirrored the concern that he had let come and pass earlier.

"Do you think he's okay?"

"No idea. But, I figured I would wait for you and we could swing by his place together, if you don't mind."

"Of course."

-

Ridley had been to Nick's place many times before. On those nights where the tourist girls had not come and Nick had not excused himself. The two men would stay late into the night, eating and smoking until such a time when Nick's age did in fact catch up to him. Ridley would help him wobble back home and put him in bed. Sometimes, after Nick's snores indicated the depth of his sleep, Ridley would sit alone in the place, relishing in the quiet that was only broken by either the old man's occasional apneic struggle for breath or a throat clearing.

Nick's apartment was not much different from Ridley's in terms of its construction, size, and layout–a fact that some time back had emboldened the young man's belief that he was on the right track.

"Clearly, if I'm already living like a real expat, I must be doing something right," he had told himself. But, as time passed and the number of nights he had carried the old man home grew, the sameness had begun to gnaw at his sense of purpose. This man was at least fifty years his senior. Returning to his own home afterward, it would feel oddly small, as if the rooms had conspired in his absence to close in and swallow him up.

Where the two men's homes most significantly differed was the collection mentioned previously. A lifetime of travel itemized and organized as personal artifacts. Hand-carved masks and idols cluttered the shelves. Original paintings he had been given over the years, sometimes for ridiculously low sums as payment for some small odd job, sat it stacks, leaning against the walls, hoping for the fulfillment of Nick's promise to find the time to hang them. Hand-woven rugs from those places once known as Persia and the Orient covered the floors of each room. His home was on par with an occult shop for the diversity of the strange, beautiful, and interesting things there were on hand to see. And, of course, every one of them had a story.

-

Carly and Ridley arrived at Nick's door about a half hour after they had set out. Ridley knocked.

"Nick?" No answer.

He knocked again, this time harder.

"Nick, you in there, buddy?" Still there was no answer.

"Maybe he's asleep," Carly offered.

"Maybe."

Ridley tried the handle and found the door to be locked. No matter. He knew where the spare key was always kept, having had to fish it out for him many a time. He unlocked the door and they entered slowly, not wanting to startle the old man, just in case.

"Nick? It's me and Carly. We got a little worried when

you didn't show up this morning. Are you all right?"

As they rounded the corner from the hall into the main room, they saw him. The old man was propped up in his favorite chair, still wearing yesterday's clothes. In his lap was an old leather journal, thick and bulging with various clippings he had shoved into it.

After a long life of travel and adventure, Nicolas Burns had died, quietly and alone in Tangier, Morocco.

Chapter 3

Unfortunately, Carly had to go back to the States before the funeral. But, in the few days they had, she did her best to comfort Ridley and help in getting things in order. Since Nick had no other family to speak of, it fell to Ridley to arrange his services. There was no will. There were no documents for bank accounts, or really any sign of how he had ever paid for anything. In the end, he couldn't afford a burial and Nick was cremated. Ridley had them place the remains in one of his old Arabian oil lamps, hoping he would have enjoyed the joke.

Using some photos she had taken the day they had met, and in the days after the authorities had removed the body, Carly was able to pitch the magazine on running a feature on the old man, using her pictures with Ridley's words. She had given them his pen name, and the powers that be were more than happy to take an article from the mind behind Rex Morgan on one of his chief inspirations.

The turnaround time was impressive and Ridley received a copy long before he was anywhere near done going through Nick's belongings. He thought on this, and guessed that they were his things at this point. They had not been left to him in any official capacity, mind you, but no one was stepping forward to dispute his claim either. Sometimes he would just sit on the floor, surrounded by the stacks of old papers, artwork, and trinkets, marveling at the task and relative ease with which a man's life can fit into so many boxes. Maybe that was why it took him so long to actually get around to doing it: a base unwillingness to reconcile that idea in regards to his own life.

The magazine had, of course, done a beautiful job assembling the piece. Carly's gorgeous full-color photos were paired with several the two of them had found stuffed into various boxes around Nick's place. Some from his wartime exploits. Others from his adventuring days. It was a fitting tribute to a truly remarkable man. A man the world may have otherwise never known that it had lost. Ridley had done his best to lay out the facts as best he was able to assemble them from the loose documents he had found and the many, many stories he had been told.

Nicolas Joseph Burns was the type of dreamer T.E. Lawrence warned us about. The kind who dreamed during the day and acted to make his dreams so. Born in the English country village of Tarraby, he served her majesty with great distinction on the African front during World War II, masterfully matching wits with General Rommel's infamous and deadly Afrika Korps, and emerging with a taste for adventure....

It went on that way, telling stories about his times in Saigon on the hunt for treasure, or in the heart of deepest Africa in search of a long forgotten medical research center. He had been paid to find an important medical file to confirm the death of his benefactor's brother. He was, of course, successful and returned to civilization with the file, and malaria, to go with it.

...Burns would eventually find himself deciding to settle in the oft hailed liberal paradise of Tangier, Morocco and live out the rest of his days as a classical English expat. He relished in any opportunity to tell his lifetime of stories, gleefully acting them out with the energy of a man half his age.

Locals all knew the kind-eyed old man with his wild stories, and would quite often pay him little mind. But, I had the pleasure to have made his acquaintance. And I can tell you that Nicolas Burns was a man with the very good fortune to live a long full life, but the equally poor fortune to have lived beyond his time. The age of explorers was some time ago, and Nick Burns truly was the last of the old adventurers.

This was the life of Nicolas Burns in so many words and so many boxes. And as Ridley sat there in the middle of it all, he couldn't help but compare his own chosen path to that of his mentor. He had wanted this life so badly when he left home. So badly. He could have damn near tasted it, as they say. "The Rogue Adventurer" as Carly had jokingly called him. That was his dream, and he had acted on making it so. But now he was faced with a clearly rendered vision of how it could end. Forced to see what came of a life lived in the solitary search for experiences. The glimpse of just what little he might leave behind was humbling and terrible, and began to haunt him.

Ridley took several swigs of a bottle of Scotch he had found beside Nick's chair. It calmed his nerves just long enough for him to set to work. The idols were carefully sorted and wrapped. The paintings were packed in crates.

When it came to rolling up the Persian and Oriental rugs, he decided to start with the one in the main room, moving the boxes aside. He turned to move Nick's favorite chair and heard a dull thud and clatter as he did so. It was the little leather book that Nick had been holding when he passed, along with a small envelope. He recognized the book for the familiar but funny looking eagle on its cover and all the clippings that threatened to burst its binding. He hadn't, however, noticed the envelope before.

He halted, unsure whether or not to go through the book. Maybe it was his journal. After a short internal debate he convinced himself that Nick would have wanted him to see it. "Just more stories," Ridley could almost hear him say. To his surprise, and annoyance, when he opened the book, it's spine cracking and unleashing small puffs of dust into the air, he found it was in German. A language with which his command was limited to ordering in bier halls. In that singular setting he was as a master, but was of little use here. The clippings themselves were in various languages. Some he could read, others he could not, but near as he could tell, they were disjointed and random. Historical essays, or articles discussing ship wrecks, or the implications of the Austrian emperor's exile to Switzerland.

He resolved to go through it later, and slipped it into his satchel where the rest of Nick's stories lived. The envelope, on the other hand, was addressed. Nick's simple, utilitarian script, clearly scratched out Ridley's name. He halted at the site of the old man's hand writing, before sliding it into his pocket. The problem of the moment was a Persian rug, and solving it demanded his full attention.

In three days he had finished. Ridley could not decide if he wanted to move Nick's things into his comparatively baron place. Would he want that daily reminder? The rent was paid through to the end of the month and he could decide all that later. With everything taken down, Nick's apartment started to feel as small as his and he decided to take a much needed walk and get out of the cramped space.

-

"How are you doing?" Carly asked.

The connection was poor but they had decided mutually that this was the best way to make their relationship work from such a distance.

"I'm fine," he lied unconvincingly.

"Fine, fine? Or, 'Please come back. I miss you so much. And, you are a golden sex goddess' fine?"

"Well, if I have to choose...."

"I know. Bad joke. Trying to make you laugh."

"I appreciate it."

He really did. Carly had been truly amazing throughout the entire process. Not just the magic she worked on the article, which could not be at all downplayed. She was strong when he could not be and understanding on the handful of occasions when he had dialed her in tears, full of fear and doubts. She knew that in the weeks since Nick had passed, Ridley's days had become far more aimless and recklessly introspective. His publisher and agent had begun sending him emails written in increasingly aggressive business speak. The deadline for the next adventure was rapidly approaching, and he knew it. But, try as he might, he couldn't bring himself to work on it. To listen to the recordings of Nick, happy as can be, telling yet another story over Kahlid's coffee.

"I have a piece in Lucerne in two weeks, but after that I can hop down to you. I'll stay as long as you need," Carly offered, with faux cheer in her voice.

"You don't have to do that. I mean, I would like it but…."

They sat in silence for a moment, allowing the long distance charge to grow. God damn it. What had he done to deserve a woman like her?

"Have you thought about maybe…moving?" she asked. He could tell it was a question that took effort for her to broach, and though it was painful, he respected her for doing so.

The truth was, Ridley had and was only now really starting to realize that it might be the best decision. But if he left, who would remember the old man? What sign would there be that he had been here and made this city his home? It was a sad and bitter burden he had placed upon himself, and it began to tear him down.

-

Carly crouched low, snapping a shot of the Kapellbrücke. She could not help but feel superfluous. It was one of the oldest bridges in the world. It did not seem a stretch to imagine that pictures of it already existed. Taken either by professionals, tourists, or Snapchatting tweens, clearly the bridge was present in the greater photographic conscious.

Why then, was she there? Because, back in 1993, some culturally and historically insensitive jackanapes had set it on fire. Carly was here to cover the anniversary celebration of its reconstruction. Was it even the same bridge at this point? Sure, much of it still stood, but nearly as much of it still had the look of freshly cut pine, even this many years later.

She snapped a few more photos before taking a deep breath of the cool Swiss air and checking her phone. Still no calls. Where was Ridley? It had been at least a week since they had spoken last and she had already made the transition from concerned to full blown panic behind her eyes. Another day, and she would be done in Lucerne and able to fly on to Tangier.

In the meantime, beer. She wound her way through the touristy shopping district and back to a small square, hemmed in by taverns on three sides. The most ornate of them, Restaurant Fritschi, was just opening and a waiter flashed a smile before waving her to an outdoor table.

"Would you like a drink?"

"Eichhof."

"Would you like to see a menu?"

"No. Thank you. Just the beer."

The waiter went in and started the pour while Carly glanced around the little square. A compass shape had been marked out in the cobblestones with smaller white stones. *For the drunk who needed to know the way home*, she mused to herself before starting to hum a familiar drinking song her father had taught her.

The Fritschi was covered in a gargantuan mural that extended just above the door frame and all the way up to the roof line some five stories above. A spiritual king spread his ghostly arms above a number of masked men, and below them, a hellfire of flower petals.

Before she could decide if she liked it or not, the beer 67

came. A large, frothy, golden mug. She checked her phone again. Still nothing. Fuck it. Let's call him. She dialed and sat there, sipping her beer and waiting for the line to connect. Voicemail. Not just voicemail, but the voicemail of a voicemail box that had not been set up yet. She couldn't even hear his voice. The universe, in its infinite cruelty, would not even grant her that.

Chapter 4

The call came in around 15:00. To Mike Kennedy,
the ringing of that particular cell phone was like a cash
register. Music to his ears. Figuratively as well as literally,
as the ringtone of choice was Pink Floyd's "Money." When
that phone rang, he knew he was in for that "good good
buuullllllshit."

He scooped it up from the bar and gave Jenny, the
bartender, a wink as she passed.

"Go for Kennedy," he said, sipping on his pint.

"Gear up. We're wheels up at 21:00."

The voice on the other end was ragged. He knew it
well. Well enough to know the story behind it. Well enough
to have ceased to be amazed that Harris could still speak after
taking a blast of shrapnel to the throat. The things they got used

to in this line of work.

"Sounds good. How many of us are going in?"

"Boss called AK Protocol."

Mike nearly spit out his beer at that.

"AK? Jesus."

"Yeah. This one looks to be pretty hardcore. Strap up, and get down here. It's pay day, Kid."

Harris hung up and left Mike to think. AK Protocol. He had heard about it as a hypothetical, but in the five years he had been with the outfit, with as much as he had seen, he never saw it put into action. The whole company, over three hundred of the world's most lethal private military contractors, being called in on one job. He smiled as he downed the last of his beer, and threw down a too-small tip on the bar.

He didn't know where he was going, but he was on his way. He pitied whomever they were up against.

–

The incessant silence of Ridley's days grew to a

crescendo and, after a time, no amount of hash or classic rock was able to abate it. He had not left his apartment in days. Instead, he was content to make his acquaintance with the budding hereditary alcoholism that he had until now only flirted with. He had danced with occasional bouts of excess and lost weekends, punctuating them with the compulsory cold turkey abstinence, typically lasting a month or so before his next drink. But this was different. He had finally unchained her and she was a cruel and vile mistress made all the more unbearable by the heat. The God damned heat! Why was it so fucking hot? Why?!

Carly was understandably worried about him. He had stopped answering her calls about a week before. The end of her Lucerne job was approaching and the two of them had never really squared away whether or not she would be coming to visit. Probably for the best she didn't, considering the shape of both his apartment and its occupant therein. His agent and publishers' emails evolved from strong words to angry, expletive-laden voicemails. Threats of lawsuits. At a certain point he had just turned the phone off. Or maybe he had forgotten to charge it. It had become hard to remember things like that. Or anything, really. Either way, he was off the grid.

Around the time he had reached the bottom of his last bottle and the morning call to prayer was a nagging drill to his brain, the random thought occurred to him that another man in the city might be feeling something at least vaguely akin to his own pain. After a quick sink bath and combing the tangles from the matted mess on his face, Ridley resolved to spend the day with that man.

-

When Ridley arrived, Khalid was overjoyed to see him. It would seem his assertion was nearer the mark than not, and in the time since Nick and Ridley had stopped coming, his business had suffered. He brought coffee and breakfast as per their usual routine, but rather than returning to the inside, he paused, considering for a moment before pulling a chair from one of the other tables. He sat down beside Ridley, pointedly leaving Nick's chair empty.

"I miss him as well," Khalid said. "He was a good man."

From anyone else it would have sounded like nothing more than pure platitude, but from Khalid it was an appraisal that seemed without contest. Nick was indeed a good man.

Ridley and Khalid talked for quite a while. At first about Khalid's wife and new baby. He had named him Saladin.

But, as one might have expected, the conversation eventually swung back around to Nick. Laughing, they shared their favorite stories back and forth until finally falling quiet an hour or so later.

"He would always come here," Khalid said. "Even on the days you couldn't. He would come and sit and write in his little book."

Ridley thought about that. He really was "it" for Nick. Somehow, with all other evidence, that was the statement that nailed it for him and he began to feel his eyes go glassy once again.

"Any more coffee?" he asked, trying hard to hide the quiver in his voice.

"I'll make more."

Khalid got up and went back inside.

Ridley took out his pencils and sketch pad and busied himself with a random stream-of-conscious doodle. Something that could almost have been a 60s Steve Ditko Doctor Strange cover, if only he had had the talent.

"Imagine my surprise…." said a raspy but powerful voice.

Ridley's eyes flicked up from his work to find a man in

Nick's chair.

"…to sit down to breakfast one morning, open my favorite magazine, and read a very nice article, detailing my entire life and very premature death."

The man, who till now had been staring at the crack in the opposite wall, slowly turned to face Ridley. He had seen that face before, but couldn't place it in the moment. Partially out of shear confusion.

"The only problem is–as you can clearly see, and much to the displeasure of many–I can guarantee you, I am very much alive."

A thick scar traced its ragged path along his right brow. It travelled down, crossed his eye, and ended and inch or so from the corner of his mouth. He was older. His greying hair was cut close and he had the baring of a man who had served. Where Nick had allowed his age to catch up to him and gone doughy, this man looked as though he had run from time and grown stronger for it.

The man extended his hand and smiled a smile that gave Ridley the vague feeling that he might have been meeting the devil himself. He took it.

"Nicolas Burns. Charmed. I'm sure."

Chapter 5

"I've read your work," the man continued, either unaware or unconcerned with Ridley's obvious confusion. "Rex Morgan is among my favorites. Trivial, of course, but great fun."

As he spoke, he reached across the table. Ridley flinched, pulling his hands away, but the man just placed his fingers on the edge of Ridley's coffee saucer and slid it, and the cup, toward himself. He reached into his pocket, removed a flask, and dropped a few drops into the cup before taking a sip. Immediately, a flare appeared behind the man's eyes, and just as quickly receded.

Ridley became aware that his jaw was working without producing sound and, with some great effort, managed to stop it. His brain was in a wild tail spin, but he got the air of danger from this man, and did the best he could to hold it together.

"To what do I owe the pleasure," Ridley asked with faux nonchalance.

"I could ask you the same thing," fake Nick countered, producing a copy of the travel mag's latest issue. He cracked the spine to a marked page and read aloud. "'From my time spent with Nick Burns I quickly came to love the man filially. A raw and true representation of the life of adventure; I had until now only grasped it in fiction.' A little overly florid, no?"

"You and my agent would get along nicely."

The man placed the magazine down and leaned in close on both elbows, swinging his body around in the chair to face him dead on. He sat appraising Ridley for a moment longer than the silence would ever be comfortable in such a matter.

"I won't beat around the bush," he said with such suddenness that Ridley had to try and conceal a slight jump. "I am a man of resources. I know you've been meeting with a man you knew as Nicolas Burns, and I knew as Carter Ponsley. What did he tell you about the book?"

Ponsley? Nick was Ponsley? Ridley knew he was going to have to back-burner that realization and process it later. Instead, he quickly cycled through his brain for any story Nick may have told him involving a book. There were old manuscripts and scrolls. Something about a hunt for the library of Alexandria. It could have been any of them.

"Can you be any more specific?"

This "new" Nick laughed to himself for a moment, took a deep breath, and faster than he could react, grabbed Ridley's arm with his left hand, flipping it over and jamming two fingers of his right hand into the center of Ridley's wrist. The pain was excruciating and he was in that moment as one paralyzed. He could feel a single bead of sweat roll down his brow.

"Let's try again. There is a book. A very small but very, very important book. Now, you are the one who has spent the last six months with Ponsley. You are the one going through his every last brick and brack. I should not think it is too far outside the realm of possibility that you would know exactly where to find what it is I am looking for. Can we agree on that?"

It took all of Ridley's effort to fight the pain long enough to nod. The man removed his fingers from his wrist, but continued to hold it in a death grip.

"Now speak," he said as though ordering a pet to do so.

It took a moment for his eyes to clear and stop watering. Once they had, Ridley saw that New Nick had pulled a knife and was looking at his arm clearly wondering the best place to start the cut. Before Ridley could open his mouth,

Khalid stepped out of the restaurant.

The man was too quick and the knife was out of his hand and in Khalid's eye in an instant. There was a wet smack, along with the scream that followed and the thud when Khalid hit the ground. Ridley turned to look, but the man smacked him with the flat side of the blade.

"No, no. Focus on the task at hand" he told Ridley. "My book. Where is it?"

Ridley could hear Khalid's screams behind him. They echoed in his head. He knew he had to say something or this man was sure to kill the both of them.

"I know what you're thinking," the man said with a very business-like tone. "You're thinking,'Someone will hear the screams. Someone will come and drive this mad man off.' But, you see. No one is coming. No one. My men are making sure our conversation stays nice and private."

He rose to his feet and calmly ambled over to Khalid, who was rapidly speaking in a mix of Arabic and shrill cries, unsure whether or not to pull the knife from his eye. The man loomed over him for a moment and Khalid recoiled. He reached for his blade and Khalid batted at his hand, trying to scramble and get distance between them.

Ridley had to do something. He had to think quickly.

There was a butter knife on the table. That would have to do. He slipped it into his sleeve.

"I know where it is!" he blurted out, half surprising himself. He turned in his chair to face him. "Little leather book. German writing." He figured it was worth a chance.

The man smiled, shifting his attention to Ridley. Khalid leaned against the door frame, his good eye darting about in terror.

"That's the one," the man replied.

Khalid tried to stand, but the man placed a hand on his chest and shoved him hard back to the ground.

"Stay here. A medic will be along shortly to look after you," he said before turning back to Ridley. "Now where is it?"

It was clear. His abuse of Khalid had clearly been just a tool to toy with him.

"Hidden," Ridley said. "But, I can get it for you."

Until now he had had no sense of scale for the man. But, seeing him standing and looming close enough to smell his aftershave, he could see he was a mountain. His age had only yielded experience. And, that experience had made him powerful, cruel, and deadly.

"Fine. You're going to take me to it."

—

The two of them made their way down the narrow streets. Ridley with his hands up, and the man who called himself Nick holding a gun to the small of his back. The streets were empty and everywhere Ridley looked, armed men lined the rooftops. They weren't soldiers. No. Judging by the plain black uniforms, body armor, and cutting edge armaments, they were more likely private security.

A movement out of the corner of his eye caught Ridley's attention, and he turned just in time to see shutters close. Whoever these guys were, they had the locals scared. The man's gun jabbed him in the lower back sharply, pressing him to go on. Who was he to argue?

They rounded the corner and Nick's apartment building came into view. There was painter's scaffolding covering its front, but no painters in sight. The whole area was deserted and the men on the rooftops stood stoically silent as Ridley and the man with the gun in his back approached.

"We've searched his home already," the man said. "Are you implying there's some subtle niche we've missed? A loose floorboard perhaps? Ponsley was always one for the theatrical."

"Yeah. Something like that." Ridley had no idea what he was going to do. Walking to Nick's place seemed like something to do at the time. He figured it would have given him time to come up with a plan. But, here they were climbing the steps and his famously lucrative imagination was coming up empty.

When they reached the top of the steps, he could already hear the sounds of Nick's stuff being trashed. Several more of the man's private security team were roughly slicing open pillows and smashing statues as they entered. They all immediately stopped when they saw their boss.

"This man says he knows where it is," said the man with the gun.

The security team stood motionless. Expectant.

"Go on," he said, pressing the gun into Ridley's back once more. "We are all so very curious."

Ridley stepped forward with his hands still up, doing his best to not make any sudden moves while still attempting to make his movements look purposeful.

The apartment was a wreck. All the boxes he had packed weeks ago were poured out and tossed around. He noticed they had moved Nick's favorite chair in front of a window. "That seems like a good hiding place," he thought.

He approached the chair and circled to its back. There was already a long slash up the back where someone had clearly searched via boxcutter surgery.

One of the unnamed men spoke up. "I already–"

Faux Nick held up a hand, silencing him, and watched Ridley intently, his gun fixed to his movements.

Ridley crouched behind the chair. He took a deep breath. The air flowing in through the open window was cool and smelled of spice. The street was silent. It was just him. Him and an unknowable number of armed men.

Ridley reached to his satchel and felt the shape and weight of the book. He could hand it over now and they would maybe let him go. But, he knew that was just wishful thinking. Besides, this book was Nick's. He wasn't about to hand it over to these guys. Honestly, since when do good guys take over several city blocks with armed men just to get a book?

"We are waiting."

A decision had to be made. The time for stalling was rapidly drawing to a close.

This is going to be very, very stupid, Ridley told himself, and leaped backwards through the window.

He landed hard on his back on the painter's scaffolding,

sheltering behind the window sill as gunshots rang out. He could see the gunmen on adjacent rooftops looking from one to the other in confusion. That was a precious resource that he would need to make use of before it ran out.

"God damn it! Go! Go!" He could hear the man shout while they reloaded.

Ridley wasn't going to waste time. Scrambling to his feet he ran for the scaffolding's edge. He could see the adjacent building. It was far, but thinking about the distance would take too long. It was jump or don't. So, he jumped.

He missed the balcony he was aiming for but landed on the floor below, feet first. When he made contact, pain shot through his legs and he thought they might have broken, but as the rooftop gunmen made him aware that they were no longer confused via unchecked gunfire, he realized he had to keep moving regardless.

Ridley threw himself through the wooden door of the balcony, and landed on the living room carpet of a small family. The smell of a perfectly seasoned and home-cooked beef tagine rushed at him and for a moment he lay there on the floor in serene confusion, eye to eye with a mother and father, and their children.

"Stay down!" he shouted in Arabic as bullets tore

through the wall, leaving beams of light in the dark room. The mother and father clung to their children, holding them to the floor. A break in the gunfire and he was up and moving on his thankfully unbroken legs.

"Sorry about the door!" Ridley threw back as he tore out of their apartment and into the hall. Curious neighbors peered from their doors and began to emerge, clogging the path. He pushed through, as politely as he could for being prey.

He took the stairs down, two at a time, and was able to emerge in an alley behind the building. Outside he was in his element. They might have had the firepower, but Ridley knew these streets. After six months of rambling around, drunk or sober, they were the nearest thing to a home field advantage he was going to get. He bolted, spurred on by the renewed cracks of indiscriminate gunfire.

-

Ridley got back to his apartment and was surprised to find it wasn't covered by Burns's mercenaries. His plan was simple as he had conceived it. He would go in, get just enough stuff to get him out of town, then follow through and get the hell out of there.

Rounding the hall to his unit, Ridley stopped dead. Carly was at his door, slamming her fist against it in an action that could only have started as a knock but grown in ferocity over unanswered time. She had a large backpack that he assumed was full of her gear from the Lucerne shoot. He didn't know what to say to her, but time was still of the essence and so he would have to walk briskly into that impending awkwardness.

She saw him. "Oh my god!"

She ran towards him and before he could get a word out, punched him in the head. Surprisingly strong for her size, Ridley had to take a moment to allow the colors to stop swirling.

"What the hell is wrong with you?" she said. "Do you have any idea how worried I've been?"

He reached out to take her by the shoulders, partially in comfort, partially to steady himself, but she shrugged his grip.

"No. Don't touch me. What have you been doing? You smell like shit."

He threw up his hands and pushed passed her.

"Carly, babe. Seriously, I'm sorry. I am very, very sorry. But, right now is not the time for this," he said.

Ridley grabbed his door knob and found it was unlocked. Carly stormed toward him as he pushed the door open. She froze. The whole apartment was trashed.

"What the hell?" she asked.

"It's been a long day," he replied, entering the apartment and quickly scanning for what he needed. Laptop, passport, clothes, and something to carry them in.

"Who did this?"

"Apparently, the real Nick Burns."

Understandably confused, Carly tried to process the details as he recounted in brief what had been happening over the course of the last hour or so. He found his Florentine leather duffle and quickly threw some clothes in it. His laptop had been smashed, but he pulled its hard drive, slipped it in a static-free pouch and moved on to finding his passport.

"Wait? What book?" Carly asked.

He fished into his satchel and pulled out the journal. "This one. I had it on me the whole time. Had they thought to search me before I made my impromptu exit, the jig would have been up. Small miracles."

Carly took the book from his hand and started to flip through it. Ridley turned back to what he was doing, but could hear her behind him muttering in German.

"Ah ha! Found my passport."

"Oh my god," she said. "Do you have any idea what this is?"

He turned to her but, before he could respond, looked up to see the red dot of a laser sight on the wall.

"Get down!"

He dove and took Carly off her feet as a burst of gunfire peppered the wall just beyond where they had both stood.

"Time to go." He crawled to the door, grabbing an old boot and shaking two large rolls of cash from it.

"Wait!" she said.

"For what?"

She crawled back across the room to grab the book from where it had landed in the fall, ignoring the uncomfortably close bullet holes that appeared in the floor around her. Book in her hand, the two of them made for the door as another flurry of gunfire filled the air.

"Don't ever do that shit again," he told her in a way that may have sounded more scolding than concerned, and immediately regretted it.

He could hear them coming down the halls. Behind them were the loud footfalls of someone entering his apartment through the windows. He grabbed Carly by the hand and ran for the other end of the hall. They rounded the corner to a dead end.

A narrow window peaked out into an equally narrow alley, maybe three feet across, but beyond it, about fifteen feet away, was a roof.

"Come on," Carly whispered loudly, climbing up onto the sill.

"What? What are you doing?" he asked.

The sounds of their pursuers were growing closer.

She wound up and tossed her gear bag. It flipped end over end and landed on the roof.

"Your duffle. Give it to me."

"What? Why?"

"No time to argue. Just give me your damn bag."

He could see in her eyes he wasn't going to win this argument. He slipped off the duffle's strap and handed the bag to her. Another strong swing and it, too, traversed the alley and landed beside her bag.

Next, Carly climbed out the window, using the uneven brickwork to brace herself and climb slightly higher. Ridley watched her with nervous urgency.

"They're coming!"

She locked her feet in place and leaned forward, lowering her left arm.

"You're going to have to trust me," she told him. "I need you to jump. Jump, grab my hand, and swing over to the roof."

He stared at her, incredulous.

"There's no way in hell you can–"

"We don't have time to argue!"

"Hey! They're down there!" They had been found out.

Ridley quickly climbed the sill and readied himself.

"This is a shit idea. This is a very, very shit idea."

"You have a better plan?" she asked.

"No," he responded begrudgingly. "Don't you dare drop me."

He jumped and grabbed her hand. Her feet slid down the wall some but she was able to keep his momentum going.

She released his hand and he went sailing through the air, but something was wrong. He fell short, just barely catching the edge of the roof.

With no time to waste, Carly did her best to move as fast as possible, pressed between the two opposing walls, finally emerging on the other side and jumping to the roof.

She landed in a hard roll, and wound up on her back. Ridley pulled himself up.

"Don't you ever, ever–" he was cut off by a volley of gunfire and the two of them dove to either side, landing just out of the gunmen's narrow vantage.

"Is this still part of your great plan!" he yelled over the repeated pop pop pop.

"It is! It's the part where we don't get our asses shot off."

"Still a work in progress I take it."

When the fire stopped she was up on her feet and moving for the next roof. Ridley didn't need an explanation. He didn't have a better plan either. Together, they jumped. Roof after roof they just had to keep moving. After their third leap a door kicked open and they were face to face with three of the mercs. They reflexively put up their hands.

"Give us the book," said Mike, the merc in the lead. "It's all we want and you two are free to go."

"You'll have to forgive me, but that sounds an awful lot like bullshit," said Ridley,

"Give us the fucking book," he said again, cocking his MP5 assault rifle. "Or, we put you down right now."

He looked to Carly, still waiting on her to make a plan. She shrugged.

They stood their frozen. No one moved. No triggers were pulled.

Rolling her eyes, Carly lowered her hands and made a dash for the nearest one.

"Stay where you–" He couldn't get the rest out. She was too quick. A jumping knee caught him in the throat. The other two mercs took aim but didn't fire, assumedly for fear of hitting their supervising officer. Ridley took that as his cue and jumped the one closest to him, wrapping his arm around his neck in a choke hold.

The remaining merc frantically switched his aim between the two of them, unsure what to do. Before he could decide, Carly got him, too. A chest shot from the downed Mike's rifle, and he hit the ground moaning.

"Hush," Carly said. "You're wearing a vest."

Ridley continued to hold his merc. He wasn't going down. Carly spun and got him in the chest too. Suddenly he went limp and slid out of Ridley's arms.

"Let's go."

"Yes, Ma'am."

They hopped two more roofs before finding a fire escape and descending. Once on the ground they took shelter in a shadowed doorway. Out of breath and still shaken, Ridley collapsed into a crouch.

"First time being shot at?" she asked.

"By someone who knew what they were doing? Yeah. You?"

She shrugged. "I cover war zones for a living, remember?"

"That where you learned to fight like that?"

"No. That was my big brother. He was kind of a jerk." She peered around to make sure they weren't in immediate danger of being discovered. His adrenaline was starting to subside and he was crashing. The shock of the last hour began to set in. Nick wasn't Nick. The real Nick wanted him dead, but not before he had handed over the book.

"The book," he managed to choke out. "What is it?"

"Let's discuss that once we get somewhere a little more mobile, shall we?"

"We are going to have to get out of town. I don't know how, but we have to leave. Go somewhere where we can lay low."

"Oh, so you do have a plan," she smirked.

He shrugged. "Honestly? I'm still taking in the fact that we made it this far. I'm out of ideas."

She considered for a moment what to do when something caught her eye.

"I have a plan," she said.

"Yeah?"

"Yeah," she continued "But, you're not going to like it."

With that she crouched low and with some effort slid open a manhole cover.

She was right. He didn't like it.

-

It ended up not being all that bad. Rather than the smells he would have expected, Ridley was instead confronted with the stale taste of air that hadn't been breathed in decades. The tunnel was all red brick and mortar, older than he could guess, and empty aside from scattered debris.

"They're water runoff tunnels," Carly went on to explain. "They keep the streets from flooding, given that the whole town is one giant hill."

"So, barring a freak storm, we're set."

She smiled at his sarcasm based coping mechanism. "Yes. Barring that."

They weaved through the tunnels, going deeper and deeper. Their only light sources were the occasional grate they passed under and the dim screen of Ridley's dying cell phone.

"Do you know which way you're going?" he asked her.

She tapped a finger to her head. "Built in sense of direction. Dad didn't want his only girl getting lost."

"And how's that going?"

She held up a finger and hushed him. After a moment he could hear it, too. The ocean.

They hurried towards the sound as though they might lose it. As they did, the passage began to lighten. Eventually they came to an opening where the rain water would have poured out into the ocean.

Ahead of them was the port. It was full of all manner of boats: private, commercial, fishing, recreation. Among them Ridley saw it: their way out.

"There," he pointed. "That boat's heading for Spain."

It was big. Smaller than the cruise ship it sat in the shadow of, but by no means a small craft. He knew it from previous trips to Spain. That was the way out. There was no doubt in his mind.

"As good a start as any, I suppose," Carly said.

"Once we're across the strait, we can catch a train to Barcelona and lay low with a friend of mine. She'll take us in no questions asked."

Carly considered it.

"It's the best I've got," he told her.

"Barcelona it is then."

Chapter 6

Out of the Medina, and in the city proper, Ridley and Carly did their best to blend in. Burns's men were out in brazen force, cruising the streets in jet black vans and Humvees, and brandishing their fully automatic weapons as though they were the local military. On more than a few occasions Ridley and Carly were forced to duck into shops or alleys as they swept the streets for them.

"Who the hell are these guys?" Ridley wondered aloud, not even realizing he had spoken. They had taken shelter in a small clothing shop and were watching as a Jeep slowly rolled past.

Carly eyed them discreetly while pretending to browse. He could tell from her face they were somehow familiar to her.

"Oh. Shit."

"What is it?"

"God damn it. I've seen them before," she said. "These guys are bad news. Private Military Contractors. The kind who tend to get brought up on war crimes charges that always seem to mysteriously go away. I came across them a couple years ago in the Balkans. Real nasty dudes. They go by 'Pandora Dawn.' Even the United States won't deal with them anymore. They're not worth the negative press they generate."

"Well, that's…not exactly confidence inspiring."

"The sooner you and I are on that boat, the better."

They were still roughly two miles from the pier, but knew that anything could happen in that distance.

"The streets are too thick with them," he said. "We're going to need a distraction or something. I really do not want to risk a shootout. Not with all these people. Not to mention our lack of guns. So, less of a shootout. More of an us getting shot scenario. I want to avoid that too, if at all possible."

They continued their slow, shop-by-shop trek along the two miles to their freedom. His nerves were starting to fray as it seemed to him that with each pass they came a little closer to being noticed. He nearly jumped out of his skin when he heard the blaring of a car horn.

A little sedan swerved, narrowly avoiding one of the Humvees, before finding a parking spot. Two tourists, a man and a woman, hopped out.

"Did you see that?!" The man was animated with anger. "That dick almost ran me off the road!"

The girl seemed to not be able to care less, and after a few more expletives, the two of them walked into a shop.

"Americans. Great," Ridley said with some slight disdain.

As someone who actually travelled, he had become familiar with the myriad variety of tourists that one might come across in any well-appointed city. The shameful truth was that American tourists tended to be the worst. Loud, boorish, and expectant of the comforts of home.

An idea came to Ridley in that moment. He got Carly's attention and made his way to the tourists' rental car, grabbing a large plaster statue from the shop table in front of it. He rationalized that whatever he did next, they would deserve it for being poor cultural ambassadors. Making Americans as a whole look bad. Well…worse.

He opened the driver's side door which had been, miraculously, left unlocked. With the butter knife he had picked up, he was able to snap off the ignition guard and pull the wire 103 leads.

He had learned to hot-wire years ago. It was a less-than-pride-inducing time in his life. Wires bare, he stroked one across the other. The starter whirred, trying hard to turn the engine over.

"Hey," Carly said tapping his shoulder. "The world's worst couple is finishing up buying their tchotchkes. You're running out of time."

"I got this," he replied. "Just one more…and…."

The engine roared to life and he twisted the wires together. From there he turned the wheel just slightly to set the car on course, wedged the statue down on the gas, and dropped it into gear.

"Go. Now!" he shouted.

The car took off one way, and Ridley and Carly bolted in the other.

"Hey! Hey!" He could hear the tourists shouting as they ran out of the store. He didn't look back. Just ran. Just kept running. There was a loud bang and crunch as the rental car impacted the Pandora Dawn Humvee he had set it gunning for.

Distraction: Done.

The rest of the way was more uneventful. They bought their tickets and found their seats. They had arrived ten minutes before the ship was set to embark. Taking a moment to breath, he and Carly had the first opportunity to really look at each other all day.

"You had me worried, you know," she offered, once the boat had started to move.

He just stared out the window. From their vantage he could clearly see where Pandora Dawn was still dealing with the car crash.

"I called you. More times than I can count. All of this, with the mercenaries, I'll give you. But, where did you go? The last three weeks. Nothing."

Ridley shifted uncomfortably in his seat. "I couldn't."

"Couldn't what?"

"This. All of this." He gestured to everything. "Life. Haven't you ever wanted to just check out? After Nick…. Not Nick, 'Ponsley,' I guess. It was haunting to see what little was left once he was gone. Everything I ever wanted to be and it all fit into a handful of boxes. It was too much."

He knew it wasn't a good explanation, or even a passable excuse. But, it was all he had.

She considered it. Mulled it over.

"I know sometimes we don't want to think of ourselves in those terms," she said. "The idea that on an actual day in the future, you will meet your maker–"

"But that isn't even it! He was a treasure hunter and a spy. A soldier and a hero. And he was my friend. Come to think of it, I don't even know if any of that is true."

"He was your friend. That much, at least, you know is the truth."

They sat quietly for the rest of the trip. The boat was full of people and anything else to be discussed would be privacy-reliant. So, they sat surrounded but alone, in the crowd.

-

The transfer from the boat to the train was relatively painless. Peeling a few bills from one of the rolls of cash he had taken to concealing in the lining of his jacket's pocket, Ridley was able to score them a private compartment. Two beds, a bathroom, and a sitting room.

Ridley stood in the bathroom, tap running, occasionally splashing his newly clean shaven face in a vain attempt to wake up from all this.

"You okay in there?"

"Yeah. Yeah, I'm fine. I'll be out in a second." He turned off the tap and dried his face. The train towels were wildly softer than anything he had felt in the past six months.

He stepped out into the sitting room and found Carly waiting for him with a concerned look. In her lap was the book.

She glanced up, fleetingly at first, but doubletook at his sudden beardlessness.

"Wow..."

"Is that a good wow?" he asked.

"It's a 'I'm going to have to get used to this' wow." she said. "You look like you're twenty."

Ridley just laughed and tossed the towel back into the bathroom.

"So, you read German?" he asked, somehow unsurprised.

It took her a second to catch what he was referring to, but she snapped to attention and lifted the book.

"Yeah. You really don't know what this is?"

"Nope. I flipped through it, but aside from the clippings, I have no idea what any of it says."

She turned the book's cover toward him.

"This," she began, pointing to the eagle, "is a Reichsadler. The Imperial Eagle of Germany. Part of their coat of arms since the medieval times. But this one specifically is a Parteiadler. A version used by only two kinds of people. Members of the original Nazi Party, or in tribute to that, members of The Wehrmacht.

She opened the book and flipped to the inside of the front cover. She read whatever it said, and from the look on her face Ridley could tell she still could not believe what she was seeing. She held it up so he could see.

A large looping signature graced the inside of the cover.

"This is the personal diary of Johannes Erwin Rommel," she said with something akin to reverence.

"Well. Shit."

Chapter 7

When he woke up, Ridley could see the sun just
cresting the Mediterranean. Carly was still asleep, wedged in
beside him on their compartment's small top bunk. It was the
first time he had seen her sleep. Every other time they had been
together, she was always up before him, or at least awake by
the time he had opened his eyes. But, here she was, curled up
and nuzzling into him.

This was the girl who took down two mercs on a
rooftop like it was nothing. You wouldn't have guessed it had
you seen that serene, childlike face or the occasional snore it
let loose. The sudden realization of how little he actually knew
about her only made him marvel at her more. Without question
he loved this woman.

Ridley got up, taking care not to stir her, grabbed the
diary, and walked into the sitting room. Finding the most

111

comfortable spot on the couch he could, he opened the diary and started to flip through. It was still German and he still couldn't read it, but he was curious to look at the various articles and inserts.

The first thing he found was a photograph. Three men dressed in gabardine safari gear stood together smiling. Behind them was an ancient temple that looked to be Indonesian in origin. One man he immediately recognized as "his" Nick. The next, he couldn't guess. But, the third was clearly "real" Nicolas Burns. Process of elimination meant the third had to be Skip. Ridley pulled the picture out and turned it over to read the thin pencil script: Borobudur, 1953.

"Hey."

He looked up to see Carly standing in the doorway wearing his shirt.

"What are you looking at?" she asked.

He held up the photo for her to see.

"That's the guy. That's Burns."

She came over and took the photo from his hand, scrutinizing it.

"Nick knew him?"

"Looks like it," he said. "I'm starting to think the

stories he told me where true after all. He just changed the names around for some reason. He was always telling me about him, Skip, and Ponsley. I'm guessing that's the three of them."

"So where's Skip in all this?" asked Carly.

"I would call that the question of the hour."

She took a seat opposite him and took him by the hand. Her soft, thin fingers wrapped around his. They were cold, but he felt reassured.

"Look at me," she said. "You and I are going to figure this out."

He didn't know why, but he believed her wholeheartedly. Whatever came next, he was glad to have her with him.

-

Their train came to a soft stop at Barcelona's Estacio de França Train Station. He had seen it before, but that was under much happier circumstances. Now the station's cavernously massive form of glass and iron felt cage-like. They were locked in, shoulder to shoulder with countless other travelers. Under general circumstances, the worst he would have been concerned about was pick pockets, or "Gypsies," as his friend would call them. Now, he couldn't help but feel like any one of these people might be working for Burns. A man with his own private army would not be above a poisoning. A simple bump and a quick poke from an umbrella or ring would be all it would take. Ridley didn't even like crowds at the best of times. Now they were decidedly more hazardous to their health.

They emerged to the street and quickly hailed a cab. Ridley gave him his friend's address and they were off.

"Have you been to Barcelona before?" he asked Carly.

"A couple times," she said. "Once for a shoot. Once just after college. Me and a few girls went backpacking. It's a beautiful city."

"It has been a few years for me, but I always love it. I remember the first time I was here, I was just so struck by the idea of a city that chose an artist, in this case Antoni Gaudí, and said 'Make us a city of the future.' That, to me, is beautiful."

As if on cue, they passed the Casa Batlló, an old tenement building that the artist had been hired to redo. Ridley had seen the photos of what it looked like before. A fairly standard six-floor brick building. But in 1904, the owner, Josep Batlló, had hired Gaudi to renovate it. Now it stood a proud and bizarre sight of indisputable beauty. Small bits of colored glass littered the front in a seeming random mosaic that brought to mind Claude Monet's water lilies. Each window opened to their own small, private balcony that looked not unlike a white masquerade mask. But, the true wonder was the roof. Gaudi had imagined it as a sleeping dragon. Multicolored, scale-like shingles covered its waving form. A single window formed its eye. The chimney was the cruciform sword, piercing its side. The interior was an even more impressive sight to behold, but now was not the time to see it.

Gaudi's Catalan modernism was evident across the city, the most famous being the Sagrada Família: a massive cathedral that was still under construction some ninety years after the man's death. Each year someone would announce the end date for construction, and each year the world took it with an Epsom-sized grain of salt.

"We'll have to come back here," he told Carly. "When we're not being hunted."

-

"So how do you know this person?" Carly asked after he had knocked on the door.

"We go way back. Back to when I was young, fresh-faced, and impressionable."

She just gave him a look and he could tell she was calling him a smart ass in her head.

The door suddenly burst open, revealing his friend, Paola Catalano. The curvy little fire ball of Italian and Columbian decent.

"Hola!" she shouted, and upon noticing Carly, immediately covered her mouth embarrassed. "You didn't say you were bringing anyone. Frickin' hell."

"Is…is something wrong?" Carly asked.

"She has chocolate on her teeth. It's a thing she does to try to make me laugh."

Paolo punched Ridley in the arm before giving him a big hug.

"Hey, Lady," said Ridley. "It's really great to see you."

"You, too."

She turned to Carly.

"And who is this?"

"Carly." said Carly, extending a hand.

Paola batted it away and pulled her in for just as big a hug.

"Nice to meet you, Carly. I'm Paola. This one has told me nothing about you."

Ridley squeezed past the two of them as Paola refused to let her out of the hug.

"Yeah, that seems to be the way of things," said Carly.

Finally, releasing her death grip, she ushered them in and up the steps to her second floor apartment.

"Come in! Come in! I just finished cooking. I did paeia, sangria, and little pinchos."

"You didn't have to go to all that trouble," said Carly.

"Pretty sure she would be cooking like that whether we came or not," Ridley told her.

Paola danced off into the kitchen. That was another thing she did. Random dancing to music that wasn't there. She was just so damn happy and full of life. He had seen her angry only a handful of times since they had met, and he had learned very quickly which side to stay on. But, as it stood now, it was nice just to be in a comfortable chair in a familiar place with the smell of saffron and seafood wafting all around him. Even if the whole place was done up in the same shade of pink.   117

"Dinner was fantastic," Ridley told Paola.

"You remember that class we took?" she asked.

"Of course. That's how I learned to clean and cook a squid."

Carly watched the two of them, sipping her sangria. It occurred to him in that moment that she had never seen him with anyone other than her or Nick. He wondered what she thought, seeing him now. Laughing and smiling so free and unguarded.

"What did you call these again?" Carly asked, picking up one of the little stacks of bread, meat, and cheese from the tray in front of her.

"Pinchos," said Paola.

"Paola doesn't eat a single meal without bread."

As if on cue, Paola immediately gasped and clutched her chest, smiling. "Oh my God! Bread!"

"See."

"So how do you two know each other?" Carly asked, attempting for nonchalance.

"Paola's a tour director. My first time on the continent, she was the one leading me and twenty-something other idiot twenty-somethings around."

Carly tried to hide her relief. "Oh. So you two never...."

"What? No!" said Paola. "I'm more...what? Big sister?"

"Yeah, I'll go with that," Ridley smiled.

"Oh!" Paola suddenly jumped up from her seat. "Do you know what we need?"

"I have a feeling you do," he smirked.

She pulled out her phone and connected it to a speaker dock.

"We need some DJ Paola!"

Carly raised an eyebrow at this. Ridley couldn't help but be amused at the pairing of the two. Carly was so calm and laid back, and Paola was decidedly not, but in the best way possible. He knew he was lucky to have them and this little vestige of safety, and almost began to forget all about Nick, and Burns, and the book. That was all back in Tangier. That was thousands of miles away.

The music kicked on and Paola immediately began dancing. Booty shaking, the tip of her tongue firmly planted between her teeth, she was happy, fiery, and alive.

He stood and allowed the beat to sway his hips as he rounded the coffee table, approaching Carly.

"May I have this dance?"

She smiled despite herself, and gave him her hand.

-

The next morning began as it always did with Paola.

"Wakey, wakey," she said in a half-shouted whisper. Ridley blinked in the sun, and turned over to see her smiling face and bushy hair poking through the door.

"There is breakfast in the kitchen when you are ready," she continued.

"You didn't have to do that. We can go out," said Carly, who was already up and dressed.

"It was nothing."

Paola smiled at the two of them and closed the door.

"She's too damn nice," said Carly.

Breakfast was composed of the basic staples of any European meal: bread, of course, meat, cheese, and coffee. Having composed his plate Ridley ventured out onto the balcony. The city was gorgeous in the morning sun. He could see the palace in the distance, and the hill where they had built the Olympic arena.

He began to wonder whether or not it would be safe to go out as Carly had suggested. Why not? They had left Tangier and Burns far behind and been careful to pay cash for everything just in case his resources reached far enough to track such things. They were, by all accounts, in the clear. May as well enjoy the town.

Ridley took Carly to the boutiques that occupied the winding little back streets and they spent the day trying on clothing they couldn't afford. Everything from retro dresses to shirts with built in LED light panels, and badass leather boots.

Not far from there, he remembered a little coffee shop he had found a time before. The term coffee shop, of course, used in the Dutch sense. The Spanish marijuana usage laws were tricky but navigable and shops, or "clubs," like these had sprung up based on a loop hole. You weren't buying weed from them. You were joining a club and donating to their cause. All of this was done in the lobby.

In the members-only section you were free to reap the benefits of membership. They provided pipes, bongs, lighters, snacks, video games, and chill music. It just happened to be that the weed you smoked was directly tied to the size of your donations. Sneaky, but still technically legal. After about an hour of this, it was time to eat.

Just off the busy and tourist-crowded La Rambla Street, across from the Jamon Experience and the Museu Eròtic de Barcelona, the entrance to the Mercado de la Boqueria was hidden down an alley that would be too easy to miss if you didn't know where to look. A massive indoor market, it housed all manner of shops. Seafood, butchers, luxury culinary ingredients at professional prices, and some truly mind blowing little restaurants, all covered in a giant roof of iron and glass.

They stopped at a shop by the entrance and for four euro picked up a little paper cone filled with Pata Negra Jamon Iberico for each of them. Thin cut shavings of ham, cut from Spanish black pigs that had spent their whole lives eating nothing but acorns. At a bite, memories flooded back of his first time Spain.

"I know where to go next," Ridley declared with
childlike delight, and quickly led Carly to his favorite little

tapas place in the market.

They took their seats at the counter and were quickly approached by a smiling barrel-chested man.

"Hola, hola. com Aquesta?" he asked, while laying down their place settings.

"Bé. Gràcies. I la teva?"

"Bé. Bé."

Ridley held up two fingers.

"Dues cerveses, si us plau. Gràcies."

He nodded and went off to grab their beers.

That was how it worked there. There was no long list of draughts or bottles. You just asked for beer and they gave you beer. Granted, he probably would have taken issue with this if it was a shitty beer, but the crisp golden contents of the glass he set in front of them never seemed to disappoint.

The counter was lined with a glass case filled with fresh seafood. On top of that case were several small plates with examples of their tapas: croquets with mushroom and cheese, peppers stuffed with crab meat, scallops on beds of sautéed mushrooms, and countless others. They ordered those three and sat, happily munching them and sipping their beers.

"This is nice," said Carly. "Not the vacation I expected, but nice."

"Yeah. I've had worse days than this," he replied with sly deprecation.

Ridley glanced down at Carly's glass and to his surprise found it already half-empty.

"I learned to drink in Prague," she said with a smile. "Down there, it's either drink or get left behind."

Without hesitation, he raised his own glass to his lips and started to chug. She saw this and did the same. Their eyes were locked as they raced to the finish. She won.

"Damn it!" he said, slamming down his still half-full glass.

She laughed, "Don't come at me with that weak shit."

Her smile shifted into something of a smirk and she reached out to trace her cool fingers along his stubbly chin.

"Missing the beard?" He asked.

"A little" she shot back, honestly. "But this guy's growing on me."

Ridley took hold of her by the shirt and pulled her close for a kiss. They relished in the moment. They were safe, alive, and together.

As they pulled apart, he caught sight of something behind her. Near the entrance of the market were two men. They weren't visibly armed, but Ridley recognized instantly that they were Pandora Dawn. One of them still bore a bandage across his nose. They were scanning the crowd and hadn't noticed them yet. He slowly turned to face the bar.

"What's wrong?" Carly asked, unclear about his sudden shift in mood.

"By the door. Don't look. There's two of Burns's men," he said.

"How did they find us?"

"I don't know," he said. "What do you think we should do?"

Carly shrugged.

"Okay then."

It was his turn.

Doing his best to seem casual, Ridley reached into his jacket pocket, peeled off a few bills, and placed them on the counter.

"I say we act like nothing's wrong, and get them away

from people. Come on."

Carly nodded and they slid from their seats and moved deeper into the market. Weaving amongst the giant fresh fish and large bowls of tiny live crabs. Deeper and deeper until they reached a section that looked as though the stalls hadn't been rented.

"There's a door," Carly said, catching sight of it.

"You! Stop! Freeze!" It was Pandora Dawn.

"Fuck! Go!" Ridley shouted.

He and Carly burst into a sprint as the bullets started to ring out, ricocheting off the sheet metal walls. Throwing the door open, they stumbled out into the blinding daylight world.

"Over there!" There were more at the end of the narrow street.

Carly grabbed Ridley by the hand and they ducked into an alley. More gunshots echoed out as they climbed on trashcans, dumpsters, anything that would support them and get them to the fire escape above.

"We have to go up!" she said.

The growing number of their pursuers left him disinclined to argue. So, they went up. And the men followed after. Once on the roof it was the run of a lifetime, hurdling chimneys and alley ways.

"Why is it always roof tops?" Ridley asked no one in particular once they had taken shelter behind a large block of chimneys.

"None of this is going to matter if they still have guns and we don't," Carly said, leaning against the chimney stack, close to the edge.

"What are you gonna–" He couldn't finish his thought before a man rounded the corner and Carly sprang into action. She jabbed him in the throat with the web of her hand, leaving him gasping while she punched his knee sideways and stole his gun.

The man floundered on the ground, unable to breath or express his pain in any way other than feeble gasps and gurgles.

"Who the hell are you?" Ridley asked.

"Come on!" Carly shouted.

"Is…is he dying?"

"He'll be fine in five minutes. We have to move."

"One sec," he said before reaching down to scoop up the merc's radio.

Suddenly, the rest of the pursuers were on them. Maybe six in total. Carly had no hesitation, popping off shots that hit some of them. Ridley couldn't count how many. One of them came for him.

Aside from the childhood martial arts classes, Ridley was by no means a fighter, and this man was clearly trained in more fighting styles than he could name, but he threw everything he had at him. He bit. He scratched. He even brought out what little Tang Su Do he could remember from the classes. It wasn't pretty. The merc dodged his every move, countering a couple and leaving Ridley gasping on the ground. He dove for Ridley but missed as he rolled out of the way. He rolled back when the merc hit the ground and swung wildly. The radio was still in his hand and he managed to bring it down right at the base of the merc's skull. He heard a crack.

The merc didn't move after that. He was quiet and still. The whole roof was. Ridley would remember that distinctly. The stillness. When he finally stood up he saw Carly, bloody but still standing. The other five men were less lucky.

"You okay?" she asked.

"I really don't know."

They got back to Paola's place while she was still out. She had given them a key and they let themselves in. Ridley was glad to not have to explain their bloodied and unkempt appearance. How could they possibly explain to the one person who willingly took them in that the danger they were running from had followed them?

"We have to leave," he told Carly after they had both showered and were changing. "You should go home and I'll just–"

"What are you talking about?" she asked.

"I'll take the book and go somewhere. But, Paola, and you…I don't want to put you in any more danger."

She looked him straight in the eyes. "You didn't do shit. This is us. You and me. And if you haven't notice I'm not entirely helpless."

"Yeah. About that…."

There was a noise. Someone was coming up the steps from the front door.

Carly immediately grabbed the gun. "Did they follow us?"

Ridley held up the radio he had pilfered. "We know

they didn't."

"Unless they know you took that."

"Hola! You guys here?" Paola said from the living
room.

Carly relaxed and put the gun down.

"Yeah. We're just…. We'll be out in a second," Ridley
said.

"Oh. I see," Paola laughed knowingly.

He looked to Carly. "We have to tell her."

-

She took it surprisingly well, all things considered. The
story of what he had been doing for the past few years, how he
and Carly had met, all the way through to running from trained
mercenaries who may or may not know where she lives.

"So, what do you do now?" Paola asked after sitting
silent for about a minute. She poured herself tea from the pink
pot she had prepared.

Carly and Ridley looked to one another and shrugged.

"Haven't really thought that far," he said. "We just know we can't stay here. You shouldn't be in danger because of us."

Paola was calm as she sipped her tea. "What about the book? Can I see it?"

He pulled it out of his satchel and slid it across the table to her. She picked it up and flipped through it.

"The men who are after you won't stop until they have this. Right?"

"They haven't come right out and said it, but yeah. That's the gist we're getting from the hail of bullets," said Carly.

Paola pulled out the photo of the three men.

"Which one is your friend?" she asked.

Ridley pointed.

"And the man chasing you?"

Ridley pointed to Burns, who's face, though smiling, bordered on a sneer.

"And where is he?" she asked, pointing to Skip.

"No idea. I mean, we know he went by Skip. But, beyond that? Nothing," said Ridley.

"Seems to me that if you really want to know what's going on, you need to find Skip and ask him."

It seemed so simple a concept and somehow up until that moment, it hadn't crossed their minds. Skip was the lynch pin to this whole thing.

Carly pulled out her phone. "I know someone who can help put an address to the name and face."

She walked off to work whatever journalistic magic it would take to dig up seventy-year-old military records. Ridley just sat trying not to look Paola in the eye.

"I didn't mean to bring this to your doorstep. I'm really sorry."

Paola considered this and shrugged. Setting down her teacup, she took his hand in a firm but gentle grasp.

"All we have in this life are our families and our friends. You did all of this because this man, Nick, was your friend. And you were all he had. He needed you and you were there. You need me, I'm here. I just hope that someone will be there for me when I need."

The words were simple. They were as warm and regarding as the woman who spoke them.

Ridley knew he had to finish what he had begun when

he set out from home that first day. He had spent a lifetime wanting adventure and here he was, being asked to heed the literal call to one. Nick. "His" Nick. His story wasn't done. Neither was Ridley's.

Chapter 8

Ridley and Carly said their goodbyes and boarded what
would be the first of many legs of travel over the course of
the next few days. It had been decided that it was important
to move in such a way that would make their trail at least
slightly more difficult to follow than the previous straight
line. They travelled from Barcelona by overly-crowded bus to
Carcassonne, France.

They were beset on all sides by elderly Spanish tourists.
Couples with some forty years of marriage behind them
chatted, argued, and snapped photos of indistinct field after
indistinct field with overly expensive and complex cameras that
they never had and probably never would take off automatic.

A medieval walled city, Carcassonne looked like
a fairytale. With its many large towers and operating
drawbridges, it supposedly inspired the designs of Cinderella's

Disneyland castle. Ridley, however, knew it mainly for two things: coffee and chocolate. Unfortunately, they were here for neither. Paola had put in a call to a friend of a friend. That third-hand friend was said to have a small plane at the nearby airfield, the kind you could ride in for a certain price. The less questions you wanted to answer, the higher the price, of course.

The two of them disembarked from the bus and joined the multi-lingual throng of flip flop/novelty t-shirt-wearing masses. The majority of the tourists stopped to take photos by the gate. But, Ridley and Carly bypassed them and entered into the human river that clogged the ten foot wide streets, letting it carry them in the direction of a small gift shop and café. Paola's friend's friend, Philippe, was meant to meet them there at ten in the morning. Checking his watch, Ridley saw they were about twenty minutes early.

"So, what do we do? Browse?" he asked Carly, already eyeing a large wood and metal carving of a knight. It held the sword in its hands solemnly, tip to the base, and hands resting on the pommel. Through the closed visor, its eyes were hard and watchful. He picked it up. Lighter than he expected. He flipped it over.

MADE IN CHINA

"I think that might be him."

Ridley followed her gaze and pointed finger to a table out on the back patio where a squat little Frenchmen reclined with a cigarette and a tiny cup of coffee. He was wearing a leather bomber jacket and khakis, and was reading an aviation chart.

"Little on the nose, isn't it?"

Carly shrugged and started to approach, doing her best to look like she was just casually starting conversation. She was good. Practiced.

"Bonjour. Philippe?"

The man waved her away without looking up from his chart. Carly stood awkwardly for a second. She turned back to Ridley, cocking her eyebrow. Ridley just shrugged.

She would not be deterred. Not yet.

"Est votre nom Philippe?" she continued.

The little man sighed, slowly folded his chart, set it down, and turned to look at her.

"Non, je ne suis pas Philippe. Je m'appelle Frédéric!"

The man went back to his chart and Carly slunk back into the shop where Ridley was making his best attempt at acting like he hadn't watched the whole thing.

"Wasn't him," she said.

"Yeah. I gathered."

"I think you are looking for me," said a raspy, nasal voice behind them.

They both spun around to find a tall, lean man in a red windbreaker and a snap brim. He looked to be in his mid-thirties. Premature grey was just starting to bloom in patches among his stubble.

"You are Paola's friends?" he asked.

"Yes. Hi. Philippe?" Ridley asked, extending a hand.

Philippe looked at his hand for a moment before shaking it. With an effortless flick of the wrist he got the attention of a waitress and the three of them were seated out back, uncomfortably adjacent to Frédéric.

Philippe wasted no time.

"I can get you to Paris," he said in a tone that seemed inarguably declarative. This was his offer. No more, no less. Do not bother asking.

He contorted his elongated form in such a way as to rest one of his legs across the other and lean back on his chair's hind legs. An action that was far from complicated, but his

angles and scale made it feel somehow wrong. A cigarette

stayed permanently locked between the fingers of his left hand, and he used it to gesticulate as he lectured them on the issues of American politics. Paola had warned this might happen and called it part of the price for an unregistered flight. Carly and Ridley just smiled and nodded. Honestly, he wasn't wrong. Though, Ridley decided it was in their best interests to not bring up the French government's shortcomings.

When his cigarette had burned down and his cafe au lait was drained, Philippe rose to his feet, without a word, and in an exaggerated movement that made him seem even more like a stilt walker. With well-practiced hands, he pulled and lit a new cigarette before looking at his two new charges expectantly.

"Alons-y."

-

Ridley had flown in a small plane many times before. His father had owned a Piper Cherokee 180 when he was a boy. Aside from that, he had ridden in a Cub over the Nazca Lines in Peru, and taken a few other less-than-legal trips in the less-watched parts of some nations' borders. Philippe's plane reminded him of the border jumpers. It was more rust, duct tape, and jerry-rig than it was actual plane. They shook and jostled over the plains of France, low enough to make out the impressively large number of vineyards. Ridley pointed them out to Carly with excitement. But, she was not taking the jostling so well, and the shaking less so.

"I could go for a bottle," Ridley said, to no one in particular.

Without skipping a beat, Philippe reached down to an old blanket between the seats and pulled it off, revealing a basket. In that moment, it was the most beautiful thing Ridley had ever seen: a bottle of Bordeaux Cab, two glasses, a baguette, hard salami, and soft cheese.

"I knew I liked this guy," he told Carly who, having gotten a whiff of the cheese, involuntarily realized it was enough to push her from nausea to full blown airsickness. Finding that they were stocked with the requisite bags, her opinion of Philippe shifted for the better as well.

Ridley uncorked the bottle, and took one sniff of the contents before reaching for a glass.

"Non, non!" said Philippe without looking back. Ridley caught a look of deep offense in the mirror. "Let it breath."

Truly, this was the only way to fly.

They arrived in Paris in time to check into a low-profile hotel in a relatively shit area of town–populated mostly by artists and prostitutes–and headed out in search of something for dinner. Generally, Ridley had found Paris to, for a lack of better descriptors, blow. He had been there a long time ago with a head full of romantic expectations fed to him glutinously by Godard and Truffaut. Lies. With the exception of the sights and the food he had been wildly let down. On the way out, someone asked what he thought and he told them quite honestly. Their response had stuck with him.

"Come back with someone you love."

Here they were and, damn it, that person had been right.

The train for London wouldn't leave until the next morning, and as Carly had finally begun to regain the color in her face, her composure, and her appetite, they decided to scan the immediate area for a little, out of the way place to drink more wine and eat more bread, meat, and cheese.

Ridley was familiar with the area around their hotel. (Honestly, more for the artists than the prostitutes.) There was a bakery down the street that sold fantastic pastries. A coffee shop the other way, run by a little deaf woman. But, just a few 141 blocks away was a shallow pocketed traveler's equivalent of a golden paradise: Restaurant le Landon Café.

He had taken refuge there in his younger days. A happy little café that embodied any and everything he had wanted from Paris. A petite corner of unshattered expectations. He and his friends had taken the place over on more than a few nights. Pulling tables together, ordering embarrassing amounts of wine, meat, and cheese, and just generally being the unabashed, young, wild, American kids they were.

He and Carly sat at a table by the window. The sun was just settling below the height of the buildings and the night began to make its presence known. People were out and about, on the prowl. But, Landon stayed quiet. Their cheese and charcuterie board came and they set to work assembling.

"The waiter."

Carly looked up. "What about him?"

"The last time I was here, he served us. Big group of us. But, he looked right through the whole group and immediately dropped to his knee and proposed to my friend Rebecca."

Carly laughed. "And what did she do?"

"Rebecca? Lived her life. Went home. Got married."

Carly sized up the waiter. "Too bad. He's cute."

A couple bottles of wine later, and they were still there. The place was still pretty empty and the staff had turned their attention to other things. As for Carly and Ridley, the talk had begun to turn to something a bit more real.

-

Part of the joy of finding someone you really connect with is that you can talk to them about anything. It can be the most trivial or heady subject. But, as much as Ridley knew he loved her, he still dreaded that their topics might dip too far in the direction of serious. Besides, they were being hunted. Who needed the added drama? But, wine does what wine does, and so they were left horny and emotionally unguarded. In Vino Veritas.

"I have to know," he said finally, after a long pause.

"Know what?"

It took him a moment, trying as hard as he could to find the right words for the question he wanted to ask. Needed to ask.

"The way you fight. You said it was from growing up   143

with a rough big brother. But, you keep taking down some of the world's best mercenaries. No hesitation. Just, POP POP POP! And they're all down."

As he spoke, he could see Carly was getting uncomfortable. But, he was drunk and he had a question. There was no stopping him now.

"Carly. Darling. I love you. But…. Who are you?"

Now it was her turn to take a moment. She took several. She also took a long swig from her glass, the whole time never looking him in the eye. Ridley began to think he may have made a massive mistake. Isn't it funny how that feeling never comes before the ill-advised choices in life?

Chapter 9

Zawiya, Libya 2011

Long before Carly was with the magazine, she was a freelancer. She didn't know anything was going to happen. There were some rumblings of course, but there were always rumblings. That was why she did the job. A valiant call to help the world separate the rumblings from the truth.

At the time, she had been married. Charles. My god, how she loved Charles. He was like Ridley in a lot of ways. Many of them she would prefer not to admit. But where she would step up to defend Ridley, Charles could handle himself, no questions asked.

He was tall, broad, strong. A real life Doc Savage, "Man of Bronze," and he was all hers.

The two of them had been shooting at the ruins in

Leptis Magna and were now headed back to Zawiya.

"Damn it!" Carly said, turning the dials of their rented jeep's radio. At first slowly, but then in a frantic twist. "This thing's busted."

Charles just smiled.

"I guess we'll just have to make do."

"No," she knew what he meant.

He kept his eyes on the road, but took one hand off the wheel and placed it on her leg.

"No," she was starting to smile and hated it.

"Iiiiiii…. I'm sooo in love with youuuu. Whatever you want to doooo is all right with meeeeeeeee…."

She couldn't help herself and burst out into laughter.

"You're so stupid."

"Youuu make me feel soooo brand neewwwww…."

He went on that way for a while.

The drive was long, and somewhere in those two hours, they switched from 1960s romantic ballads to 1990s best of grunge.

They were well into a Nirvana deep cut when they

finally rolled into Zawiya. Their timing was, in all honesty, amazing. Had they left a little later, gotten a flat tire, or even stopped to let a heard of cows pass, they probably would have missed it. But, no. They were right on time.

They hadn't even been in town for ten minutes before Carly noticed something was wrong.

A woman stepped out into the road, her child clasped tightly in her arms.

"Jesus!" Charles shouted, slamming the breaks and pulling the wheel hard to the left.

The woman didn't seem to notice. Carly saw panic in her eyes as she ran as fast as she could.

"Are you okay?" Charles asked Carly.

"Yeah," she said. "Yeah, I think so."

But, something caught her eye. There were more people running. All around them. The other cars had stopped, abandoned by their drivers.

"What the–" Carly began, but before she could even finish her expletive, the bombing started.

The building to her left exploded. The force lifted their Jeep to one side as rubble and dust showered around them. The blasts continued on ahead of them as the bomber laid down its

149

horrific payload.

"Carly! Carly!" Charles was shouting but her head was still ringing, her vision still a pained blur.

"Carly! Oh, God. Please wake up. Please!"

She shifted.

"What…what did…." it was a struggle to get her words in anything resembling the right order.

"Carly. Babe. I need you to get out of the car."

She touched her hand to the side of her head. There was wetness there and it stung something fierce.

"Listen to me!" Charles's voice was strange. Raspier than usual. "You have to get out of the car."

She finally turned to see him. The Jeep was on its side. The only thing holding her in place was her seat belt. Charles himself looked perfectly fine. A bit dirty, but fine. But she noticed some of the dirt was darker than others, and that the darker was mostly localized around his right arm which was pinned between the Jeep's door and the ground.

"Oh my god!" She snapped to attention and undid her seatbelt, bracing herself so that she wouldn't fall on him but rather step around him.

"The windshield," he said. "Kick it out."

It took a couple tries but on the fourth or fifth kick, the glass broke free in one large, spidery, shatterproof piece.

She climbed through and was immediately hit by the devastation. People who, seconds ago, had been living their daily lives were now dead, wounded, or screaming in agony for those who were. The air was full of smoke and dust, and the fires all around lit the world in blood red.

"Okay," Carly said, turning back to Charles. "I'm going to get you out."

"No. Carly! Just go!" he pleaded. But she was already bracing her weight against the Jeep's hood, trying hard to push it back over. Her adrenaline-augmented strength gave it a slight lift, but not enough to matter. The Jeep wasn't going anywhere. Neither was Charles.

"Carly. Darling," Charles said in a calm voice. "I love you. But, I need you to go."

"No!" she objected. "No! No! No!"

She screamed, pounding on the Jeep's hood.

"I need you to go," he repeated.

She dropped down to a crouch.

"I can't," she said. "Charley, I–"

But, before she could finish, she heard it. She stood, and just through a break in the crimson smoke, she saw the shadow of the bomber that had done this. That had blown this ragged hole in her life. It loomed, dark and bat-like. And it was coming back.

"Carly, go! Now!" he shouted. "Go!"

She leaned in and kissed him one more time. One last time.

"I love you," she told him.

"I love you, too."

With that, she turned and ran. The roar of the jet engine was growing louder and she could hear as the first few bombs began to fall. She took cover under the balcony of a nearby apartment building, looked back and saw Charley still in the Jeep. For all the stoicism he had put on for her, he was fighting with his own arm, screaming and cursing as he pulled at the broken and shredded husk that was left of it. He didn't want to die.

It was too much. To hell with her life. What would it be without him? She started to run back for him…a shell dropped nearby. The blast took her off her feet and she was thrown.

Hours later, long after the bombing had ceased, she woke up bruised and bloody, half buried in what had once been a falafel shop. All around her, people were working to dig her free. Asking, in Arabic, if she was all right. She tried to look for where the Jeep…where Charles had been. But, the landscape was changed. Unrecognizable. Everything was gone.

Chapter 10

Ridley watched her as she told the story. He could tell she'd told it before. Enough times that she was able to stop the crying. The tears were still there. Just skillfully held back. Only peaking at the edges. Her eyes were glassy and doll-like.

"I got home and decided to start taking self-defense classes as a way to distract myself. Self-defense turned into offense. Krav Maga, Muay Thai, anything. I got obsessive. Anytime I thought of him, even read his name, I would practice until I was literally sick. Until I couldn't think anymore. Until I was too exhausted to cry anymore. Until my body refused and I crumpled.

"When I lost him I was helpless. I don't ever want to feel that way again. So…yeah. That's who I am."

Ridley didn't know what else to do but hold her hand.

He reached for it, but she recoiled. Eye contact seemed out of order. So, they sat there quietly.

Gerard Lenorman played on the restaurant's radio. "Voici les Cles."

-

Drunk and emotional, they paid their bill and headed back to the hotel, walking separately, their hands thrust deeply in their own pockets in protection from the unseasonable cold. Ridley had opened his big mouth once more and got an answer he didn't know what to do with to a question he knew he never should have asked. He kept his eyes focused on his feet and the stone-paved sidewalk, only occasionally lifting them to her in search of something. He didn't know what. She never looked at him. No matter how much he silently pleaded for the most fleeting of glances, she never looked at him.

By the time they had traversed the few blocks and made it back, he had resigned himself to just focusing on getting ready for bed. The one bed. It had suddenly become a delicate danger zone. He decided it would best if he took up as little of it as possible.

Shortly after he had climbed in and found a near-comfortable balance on the bed's edge, Carly came out of the bathroom, continuing her newfound practice of avoiding the sight of him, and sat on the other edge of the bed. It seemed to him the classiest thing he could do would be to pretend he was asleep.

"I know you're faking," she said.

Damn it! When he rolled over and opened his eyes she was facing him.

"Are you okay?" he asked, half dreading the answer.

"Yeah. I just…." She paused, once again searching for the words. "I try not to think about Charley. Like all the time. It is a constant effort to not think about him. About… what happened. But, I know I'm as over it as I'm ever going to get. And more than anything else, it taught me something. I can lose. I can lose a great big part of me, of my heart, and keep living. I will always hurt. I will occasionally cry in the bathroom. But, I am here. In every way I can mean that. I am here."

She placed a hand on Ridley's cheek, softly running her fingers along it. He could feel a tear starting to brew in the corner of his own eye. But, he was too busy staring into hers to care. Those glistening gorgeous eyes. She swung her body around and leaned in, kissing him. Her hand moved from his cheek to his hair, while the other took hold of his waist.

"I love you," he said.

"I know."

And that broke it. The tension and passion was no match for the cheesiness of a Star Wars reference. They both laughed. Hard. They needed it. But, as the laughs fell quiet again, it was Ridley's turn. He took Carly in both of his arms. He kissed her. He held her close. He would never let her go.

Chapter 11

The Eurostar from Paris to London was fairly uneventful. They mostly spent the two-and-a-half-hour ride drinking champagne and splitting a Toblerone. Why the dining car stocked champagne, Ridley could only wonder. They arrived at St. Pancras station, taking just enough time to grab a coffee and a sausage roll, and hailed a cab for Paddington station.

Carly's contact in the ICIJ (International Consortium of Investigative Journalists) had somehow managed to find Skip. Miraculously, he was alive and living in a little town called Polperro in Cornwall in South West England. It was going to be a minimum five-hour trip. Carly offered to find snacks for them and something to occupy their time, so Ridley sat with their bags in the waiting area.

It had been years since he had set foot in Paddington

station. Yet, here he was, thinking the exact same thing that his fifteen-year-old-self had thought. *I wonder where they found the bear.*

When Carly returned it was with a bag full of food and a stack of paperbacks.

"Get anything good?" Ridley asked.

She tossed the bag into his lap. It was full of sandwiches, cheese, and deep at the bottom, beers that he knew they would be thankful for around the halfway point of the ride.

"What about those?" he asked, pointing to the stack of paperbacks as she sat down.

A sinister smile graced her lips and she held up the book on the top. Ridley's stomach dropped immediately.

"You didn't."

"Uh huh," she replied, still smiling.

In the Valley of the Tombs. Book one of the Rex Morgan adventures. The original. Far from the proudest thing he had ever written.

"Somehow, I have never gotten around to reading these. I feel like I probably should. I mean you have been, y'know, inside me."

Ridley swallowed hard.

"One: there are children present. Two: give me that!"

He swiped the book from her hands and started flipping through. He had not even set eyes on a copy in over three years. He turned to the dedication. *For Madeline.*

"Who is Madeline?" Carly asked playfully.

"A girl."

"Yes. But, clearly a special girl. A girl special enough to warrant a dedication in your first novel. Was she pretty? Was it love at first sight? Was she a Libra? Inquiring minds want to know."

Ridley hesitated. The very sight of that name sent a rush of discomforting warmth down his spine.

"She was a girl in my office," he said. "From my younger, more oblivious days. Our cubes were adjacent. She read a lot, and I had written a few things here and there. So, I figured I could write a novel and it would impress her."

"And how'd that go?" Carly asked.

Ridley shrugged. "She though it was sweet.Which is the best I really could have hoped for I guess."

Carly's smile faded. She noticed he hadn't looked up from the page the whole time.

"Hey," she said.

He glanced up.

"It may not have gotten you that girl." She stood while talking. "But, you did get *the* girl."

She leaned in and kissed him and he couldn't help but smile. It was true. He had.

-

They got off the train in Liskeard. The station was small, quaint, and intrinsically British. It looked like it had fallen out of a Victorian story book. A short little building. All white with red doors and gingerbread around the awning. Across from it sat a pub. The Old Stag. All grey stone and concrete window frames. The building looked older than our nation. Instinctively, Ridley raised the idea of grabbing a pint but their bus was already pulling up.

They hopped the seventy-three to the eighty-one, changing in the midst of the rolling green hills of the Cornwall countryside. The roads curved along those hills, hemmed in on either side by low hedges or stone walls. On more than a few occasions, the little old couples in little old cars that made up the opposing traffic were forced to stop and reverse for a hundred feet or so until they could back into a break in the hedge or wall, making way for the much larger bus. This was the normality of country roads here. Never a grumble or a curse. Just an unwritten understanding.

It was a little under an hour when they came over the hill and could see Polperro: a sleepy little fishing village that time had long since forgotten. So unassuming in appearance one might never guess that it had been a haven for smugglers in its younger, wilder days. It was later in the day by the time they arrived, and the fishing boats were returning with their day's catch. Organized in single file, they slipped through the narrow inlet and into the port.

The eighty-one bus stopped just outside the town proper. Founded in the thirteenth century, the town was not exactly built with cars in mind. As a result the streets could not handle them, and beyond a certain point Polperro became a walkers-only town. Some of the buildings sat at awkward angles, propped against one another with old beams. Randomly you might come across a bridge traversing one of the many streams that flowed through, unimpeded on their journey to the sea. The whole place had that heady aroma of sea spray and grassy fields. Heaven.

"Okay," Carly said pulling her notebook from her pocket and flipping to the right page. "Sydney "Skip" James apparently frequents a place called The...really? The Ship Inn. A little on the nose, no?"

"Sounds like a happening place."

"I'm sure it's where all the young, tragically hip, twenty-somethings go."

It wasn't hard for them to find. They hadn't walked long before the old wooden sign bearing a tall ship in a storm came into sight. Inside, the place, Ridley thought, was like a dream he had had once. Low light, wooden tables and chairs, and the smells of beer and seafood wafting around. The vibe felt as though pirates could burst through the door at any moment. Either that or the Doctor and the Brig could be out back fighting some menace from deep space, once again narrowly sparing the world from a working class British apocalypse.

Ridley and Carly found themselves a booth in the back and scanned the menu. Rather, she scanned the menu. Ridley knew his order.

"I'm in a fishing village on the coast of England. There's only one thing possible to order. Fish and chips with mushy peas." He told this to the waitress along with Carly's order of a shepherd's pie, and two pints of lager.

Once the food arrived and they were half-finished and completely satisfied, they began to scan the crowd.

"Do you see anyone who might look the part?" Ridley asked, pulling out the old photograph.

As if on cue, the door opened and a little old man entered. Of the three men pictured, he had clearly aged the worst. Dressed in a well-loved old tweed suit and a snap-brim, he shook as he made his way across the pub. He was crooked. His knees permanently bent as though readying to jump. He was slow, but determined, and had probably walked this same path countless times before. The cane in his left hand never touched the floor, only hovering a few inches above, either out of an old man's defiance in the face of time or the inability for his arm to reach that low.

"Alright there, Skip?" called the Bartender.

Skip just smiled and gave him as much of a wave as he could without losing his concentration on staying upright. Finally reaching his destination, the old man dropped down into a chair at a lonely corner table. The waitress brought him a pint, and he immediately set to packing his pipe from a bag of tobacco in his pocket. Just like Nick. Or Ponsley, rather.

It struck Ridley. Nick was the man who came home

from the war, chose adventure, and never looked back. Burns clearly did the same, and it turned him into something dark and twisted. But Skip was the man who came home to stay. He had had his adventures. Had his fun, and once he had had his fill, came home. It would seem life was simple for him now. A pipe and a pint and all the ills of the world would just fall away.

Ridley tapped Carly's hand and gestured to the old man, before standing and slowly making his approach, doing his best to not tremble himself.

"Excuse me," he said.

Skip looked up from lighting his pipe, and waved out the wooden match.

"Yes?" his voice was a soothing rasp.

"Is your name Sydney James?" Ridley asked.

Skip smiled. "No one calls me Sydney. Not anymore. Not since the war."

He stuck out his trembling hand.

"They call me Skip."

Ridley shook his hand and was instantly surprised to find a strong grip.

"I'm a friend of Ponsley's."

Skip's face slid from a smile to something else. At best read it was a mingled mix of sad amusement at memories past.

He sat there considering this for a moment, puffing on his pipe like an old steam engine.

"In that case, you had better sit down."

-

Chapter 12

The legend was that a diamond, once owned by
Alexander the Great, was up for grabs. It had been the eye of a
giant peacock statue in one of his regional palaces. Supposedly,
it was the size of a child's fist. Ponsley wouldn't stop talking
about it.

"It'll make us rich," he would shout. "Rich beyond our
wildest dreams!"

Skip and Burns would, of course, give him flack for
it. They had rules about the treasures they hunted. A certain
amount of researched evidence was required before the group
would go to a vote. But, if they were honest with themselves,
they both spent more than a few nights talking like school
boys. Dreaming about all the things they would buy with their
shares.

Burns was always a bit rough. Pleasant enough, but every time you looked at him, in the quieter moments, he would be off by himself. And in his eyes, you could see the wheels turning. Which came in handy on more than a few occasions. It was not uncommon for them to make it out of a tough scrape by the skin of their teeth on his wit and will alone.

It was the summer of sixty-eight when Ponsley finally found the manuscript that pushed his idle conjecture to a solid enough theory to act on, and, within days, the Englishmen were up in the hills north of Thrace, not far from Istanbul, looking for that diamond. "The Peacock's Eye."

Skip was, at the time, still upset that Ponsley had managed to pull this job together in time to beat out his Minoan Labyrinth expedition. But, by now, they had been following the river for three days. It was rough water. Rolling and churning like a pot on the boil.

When they had finally reached the spot marked in the manuscript, it was at the foot of a sheer rock face, extending a few hundred feet in every direction. No problem. Nothing they hadn't dealt with several times before. But, of course, that is exactly the kind of sloppy thinking that gets you in trouble.

"We'll have to belay," said Ponsley. He was excited as he pulled a large coil of rope from his pack.

Burns and Skip looked to one another in uncertainty, but shrugged, strapped on their harnesses, and tied on to the line.

They proceeded up the cliff one by one, nailing their pitons into the rock, and tying off. The idea of course being that if by any bad luck one of them happened to fall, the other two would be anchors. The shock of the sudden stop would still nail them right in the ghoulies, of course. So, it would be a life saver, just not the most pleasant one.

It was slow going, to be certain, but for all any of them knew, the treasure of the ages was at the top. So, they climbed. Words were sparse, used only to coordinate their movements or, every once in a while, remind one another of some bawdy story, just to break the tension.

At some point though–they must have been two-thirds of the way up–Skip missed a step.

Skip had always been the stronger climber of the three, so he had been at the lead, with Ponsley and Nick following on behind him. But, he missed that step and went down like a stone.

"Skip!" shouted Burns.

Ponsley could only watch in horror. He may have just killed his friend.

But that's what the pitons were for. Skip braced himself for that shock but, when he reached the first one, the rope snapped like twine. Ponsley did his best to catch hold, the rope rapidly sliding through his hands, but in the end it was Burns who swung out and grabbed him.

They hung there for a moment, twisting.

"I got you," Burns said. "I got you."

"Much obliged," said Skip, with a smile and a slight laugh, as he did he best not to look down.

"You two all right down there?" Ponsley asked. His hands stung from the rope burn, but he still clung to the cliff.

Burns looked up him, with thinly-veiled disdain. "We're fine."

But between the swing and the combined weight of the two men, Burns's rope started to fray as well.

"Good lord," Skip managed to get out through gritted teeth.

"Go. Go!" shouted Burns.

Skip dug his hands into the rock until he could support himself and Burns could go back to focusing on his own ascent. They would have to free climb the rest of the way.

Ponsley reached the top first and disappeared over the edge. Typical climbing decorum says the first one to the top would lend a hand, but he was gone, and Burns cursed his name the whole rest of the way.

When Skip and Burns finally got up and over, they found where he had gone. He was just sitting there, staring. Twelve o'clock half struck, as one might say. The library was, of course, more beautiful than any of them could have guessed. It was massive, gorgeous, carved into the rock face, and on the opposite side of the ravine.

It was set back far enough that you couldn't see it until you reached that height. Just beyond the lip of sight until then. Brilliant. Deviously designed, Skip had to give them that, but his moment of mystification was short lived.

Burns dove at Ponsley, cursing him something fierce. In truth, conflict between the two men had been building for years. This was just the culmination. Though the Library's side of the ravine had a grand open space before it, all colonnade and statuary, the ledge they were standing on wasn't nearly wide enough for the two of them to be rolling around and scrapping as they were. But, of course, they didn't care. Decades worth of animosity and aggression were playing out.

You can probably guess what happened next. Burns laid into him, throwing punch after punch, not pulling them in the slightest. Ponsley took them until he found his opening and got one good kick square in Burns's chest.

Burns went over the side. As fast as it happened, when he looked back, Skip could still remember the look on his face. He wasn't surprised. He wasn't even scared. He was just… angry. Fiercely so. There was fire in his eyes as he went off to meet his maker.

He was still attached to Ponsley by the belay rope and the two of them grabbed for it instinctually. But, it wasn't meant to be. The rope, already frayed from the earlier strain, snapped and Burns dropped. It felt like he fell forever. Then he hit that roiling water and was gone.

Ponsley and Skip went their separate ways not long after that. The library had turned out to be a bust in the end, and at a certain point Skip decided that he had had enough of all that. He had lived a life he could be proud of and been lucky enough to survive it. Seeing Burns go, it put things in line for him. It was time to come home. The last he had heard from Ponsley, he was off somewhere in Bali, still searching. For treasure. For something.

Chapter 13

Ridley and Carly stayed the night in Polperro. Feeling his age, Skip had turned in for the evening, but not before all agreed to return the next day. Since meeting the real Nikolas Burns, Ridley had, of course, begun to wonder about all that Nick had told him. At bare minimum, knowing he wasn't even who he had claimed to be had cast his stories into a realm of incredulity. But, there was a comfort in hearing Skip tell them.

There were of course slight differences, as one would expect. The long bleary hand of time had wiped away some of the details in Skip's memory, not to mention the inherent differences of perspective between the two men. But, they were similar enough that Ridley knew Nick, his Nick, Ponsley, was the man he thought he was. If not in name, then in deed.

Carly booked a room for the two of them in the Inn above the pub. It was warm, wooden, and smelled of must

179

and the sea that their window overlooked. Ridley exited the bathroom to find her sitting in the dim light, deeply enwrapped in the little leather book.

"Anything interesting? Was Rommell in the midst of a torrid affair?" he asked with an air of what had recently been referred to as his "lovable jackass-ishness."

She didn't stir. Her brow was deeply furrowed as she turned the page, then quickly back, then forward again, as if comparing.

"What is it?" he prodded.

"I don't know." She held up the book so he could see. "This word here. 'Zerzura.' It's not German. It's not any language I know. The first half of this book is just boring military jargon, but suddenly, anything and everything revolves around this word."

She marked her page and handed Ridley the book to see. All the inserts Nick had filled it with had been removed and spread out on the room's desk, subtly numbered so they could return them to the appropriate pages if need be. Carly got up to check them as he scanned the book for anything he could read.

She was right. Over and over again, the same word popped up. Always written in such careful, light script as though the author had held the very action in reverence. "Zerzura." Why did it sound so familiar?

"I feel like it has to be a name," Carly said, still squinting at the little scraps of paper and random indicia.

"What makes you say that?"

"The syntax. Rommell talks about having 'found Zerzura.' Or the 'love of Zerzura.'"

"So, he *was* having an affair," Ridley half joked. It didn't land.

"No. Honestly, I think it might be a place. Look in the back."

He flipped through the book until he came to a foldout section that contained several doodles and words in German along with the recognizably reverential script of Zerzura.

"What is this? A map?" he asked.

Carly shrugged.

"Seriously?" he continued. "Are we seriously thinking that we're being hunted for a map? The type of map one might assume leads to treasure? Is that a thing we're thinking now? Because that would be a thing that crazy people would think."

Carly shrugged again. "Do you have another

suggestion?"

"Yeah. One. How about we wait till we ask Skip about the book before we start looking for the 'X' that marks the spot?"

He was clearly trying to play it overly cool. Why would it not be a treasure map? It realistically made just as much sense as everything else that had happened in the past few days. Real people did not get chased by mercenaries, or find lost World War II relics. That just didn't happen in real life. But, the fact that they were hiding in the upstairs of an English countryside pub, at the furthest edge of that chain of events, made him start to reconsider what one might regard as normal or real.

"I'm not sure we can entirely trust him," Carly said after a long silence.

"Skip?"

"Yeah. Something about his story bothers me."

"Aside from the fact that Burns isn't dead?" he offered.

She considered this.

"No. That I'll allow. A fall like that into a river, as long as he missed the rocks, there's no reason that would necessarily kill him. But, if they never found any sign of a body, it would be understandable for them both to think he was dead. Probably why Nick took his name. Some kind of penance. A tribute."

"Then what do you think it is?" Ridley asked.

"The climbing," she said. "That part of the story doesn't really make sense. For one, these guys were all experienced climbers. No way would they have cheaped out on the rope for an expedition like that. Plus, Skip says it snapped under his weight when he fell, but when Burns swung out and caught him it held the both of them, just fraying a little bit."

"Why would he lie?"

"I don't know. But, I think there's something else going on."

-

"He's late," said Carly.

She was right, of course. And, of course, it began to seep into Ridley's mind that they may, at that point, be so unlucky as to have another old man die on them, just short of telling one last story. Was it a fucked up thought? Sure. But he thought it nonetheless. Aside from the obvious issues of natural causes at his age, what if Burns had caught up to them?

183

What if the two men had had a secret late night confrontation after Skip had returned home from the pub, finding Burns sitting in his comfiest chair, armed with a revolver? What if they had one last talk about the old days, heavily laden with in-jokes and references lost on any passing ear? What if Burns had put down his old friend just to keep him from talking to them?

"There he is," said Carly, stirring Ridley from his internal musings.

Skip made his way across the pub in much the way he had the previous day. Giving waves and greetings, shaking all the way, and coming to rest at their table.

"Did you bring it?" he asked knowingly.

Ridley had begun to appreciate his lack of small talk. Surely, he realized how little time he had left and the prudence of speaking plainly in waning days. Ridley took out the old book and slid it across the table.

Skip placed his hand on its cover. For the first time since they had met, the old man was still. His hand felt the grain of the leather. His fingers remembered this book. After a moment, he pulled it towards him and, without opening it, placed both hands on top.

"I never thought I would see this again," he said with a

quiver of emotion in his voice. "You know what it is?"

Carly and Ridley nodded.

"And who it belongs to?"

They nodded.

"Where did you find it?" Ridley asked.

A tear began to form in the corner of Skip's eye. A tear that hadn't been there when he told the story of Burns's supposed death. He felt it there and wiped it away before continuing.

"We found this book in the one place you would expect for it to be. We found it on Erwin Rommel's night stand," he said with an emotion-laden smile.

-

Skip was twenty-three at the time. He, Ponsely, and Burns had been running routine odd jobs around their station. As just a few among Prince Albert's own 11th Hussars, they had taken the Italians' Fort Capuzzo in a blaze of glory, but were now relegated to patrols, scouting, and supply runs. Really anything you could ask of a Jeep crew outside of combat.

Together they accumulated all manner of stories about being caught under heavy fire, or going head to head with the Luftwaffe with little more than a fifty caliber and the grace of God. But, in truth, those were the few and far between. Ever since that last big push, they were rarely in the thick of it. Sure. They would have the occasional run in with an enemy scout, but the vast majority of their days on the front were spent in unending boredom in the god forsaken heat, staring at an endless sea of sand.

Like any other day, they had been sent out to scout. It was a further quadrant of the grid than they would usually look to, but orders were orders, so they fueled up, kicked the tires, and got on their merry.

It was round about midday when they stopped for a rest, pulling into the shadow of a dune that towered high as a hill. But, as big as they were, you could just watch the wind move them like God's hand to a mountain. Just a massive form, scattered to dust.

They ate their rations, drank their canteens, and even slipped a few sips from a bottle Burns's sweetie had sent him. When the sun started to crest the top of the dune, they looked to one another and decided it was time to move on. Only problem was that when Ponsley got behind the wheel and gave the key a turn, nothing happened.

186

Nothing. Not the repeated whine of the starter. No indication the engine was even attempting to turn. Nothing. Ponsley cursed her something fierce before hopping out and popping the bonnet.

"Bloody hell!" he shouted.

"What is it?" Burns asked.

He and Skip climbed out and rounded on the engine to take a look for themselves.

"There's no water in the battery!" Ponsley went on. "And look! The plates are corroded!"

"What does that mean?" Skip asked. "Can we just pour some in from the canteen?"

Ponsley sighed and walked away.

"Well?" Burns asked.

"No we can't pour it from the bloody canteen!" Ponsley shouted. "Even if the plates weren't corroded, the water needs to be distilled."

"What does that mean for us right now?" Skip asked.

"It means we need to start walking."

The three men pulled all the food and water they could carry without weighing themselves down too much. There was a long debate about whether or not to unhook the fifty caliber and bring it along. Would the weight of it be worth it if they were to run into Jerry along the way? In the end it was decided to err on the side of mobility and rely on their side arms if it came to it.

They did their best to plot a course on the map, but with literally no distinguishing land masses it quickly seemed foolish. All they had to follow was the sun. What they did not have was shade. Water ran low quickly. This was not the way it looked in Lawrence of Arabia. There was no grand score. This was desperation in the heat. Madness in the baking sun.

When night fell, the men were granted a temporary reprieve from the heat, but as had often been said, the desert can be like a man without a woman. Hot by day but cold by night. The temperature dropped to near freezing and the three of them were forced to huddle closer than decency permits in aid of survival through shared body heat.

Two days they were out there before they caught sight of anything. Of course, by then, the three lost soldiers were suspicious of anything they saw. Skip himself had caught sight of a few too many glimmering pools that turned out to be mirages, or lights that were never there. So, when they came across the camp, they approached it with suspicion, and eventually disbelief.

They crouched low behind the edge of a dune, less out of covert strategy and rather due to their inability to stand at that point. It was night time, but Skip noticed it first. The flag flying overhead wasn't British. They had stumbled out of hell and onto the doorstep of the enemy, Jerry's swastika mocking them from thirty feet up.

"What do you want to do?" asked Ponsley. "Because, I haven't come this far to lay down for these fascist bastards now."

It might have been the dehydration that emboldened him, but he was right, and Burns and Skip said as much. The first step would be forming a plan. The camp was surprisingly small, and clearly temporary, as it was made up entirely of tents and guarded with foot patrols. They knew they had to be scouting for something.

Mustering what little strength they had, the three men circled around the edge until they had gotten a good lay of things. There were five tents in total. A barracks, a mess, latrine, command, and meeting.

189

Water would need to be priority number one. Food, if they could find any, would come second. After that, transport. The huns had a fair number of Jeeps parked all pretty and waiting to be taken for a spin, and Skip could see Ponsley was already eyeing them like prime rib.

They moved in on the mess tent from the rear and Burns was just about to pull the flap back when he heard someone coming.

"Get down!" he said in a constrained, but forceful, whisper.

When the German stumbled out drunkenly from the barracks, they were already hidden, having taken cover behind some scattered crates. They watched as that Nazi bastard found a little out of the way spot to drain his willy. He was singing "Oh Mine Papa" before Burns crept up from behind, and used his service knife to put some moonlight into his neck. A hand over the mouth to muffle the scream, and the rest was bloody history. Burns let him go, and the body tumbled down a dune and into its shadow.

He cleaned his knife in two quick swipes against his trousers and motioned for the other two to follow.

They made their way into the mess tent and looked in vain for the water tank. The Jerry must have locked it up that late in the night, though Skip did find the basin where they were doing the washing up. It was tepid and smelled like a whore's business, but as far as the three of them were concerned it tasted like the choicest wine. They drank it all till their bellies were full and they sank to the ground reeling. They sat there for a while, smiling like fools and laughing under their breath at the ridiculousness of the situation.

"The way I figure it," Burns began in a whisper, "We're already here. May as well have a bit of a look around. See what we can see."

Neither Skip nor Ponsley could find much of an argument to counter with.

"No harm, I suppose," said Ponsley.

From their earlier reconnaissance, they knew there were six krauts running about the place on patrol, not counting the one Burns had ventilated. If they were quick and quiet, it wasn't outside possibility that they could make their way around them to the command tent, grab whatever intel was on offer, and get on out without raising an alarm. There was no guessing how many of the huns were packed in for the night, and it was generally agreed to be best not to find out.

They shimmied on their bellies for most of the way, crawling through the sand and sticking to the shadows, occasionally rolling clear of flashlight beams as was needed. It wasn't long before they were at the back of the command tent, using Burns's knife to slice their way in.

It was the mother lode. Charts, reports, everything you could want. And to cap it all off, Erwin Rommel, the Desert Fox himself, was sleeping on a cot in the corner.

-

Skip faltered a bit here. Ridley could tell he was in the midst of several emotions. What he could only assume was the experience of recalling a long dormant memory, and all the complex feelings that went with it.

"Why didn't you kill him then?" Carly asked, stirring the old man back to the present.

Skip smiled to himself. He suddenly seemed, somehow, much older. Frailer.

"I asked myself that question quite often in the years that followed," he said. "We were kids. Even Burns, his blade at the ready, couldn't think to put an end to him. It would be like putting down the boogie man. He had been tormenting us for months, but there he was, sleeping like a man. Like any man. We grabbed everything we could–maps, charts, documents–hot-wired a Jeep and got out of there. The alarm was raised, but we were too far off by the time any of the huns was awake enough to chase after."

-

He went quiet again after that. Ridley could tell he needed to sit with that story. That he needed to let it lie.

Again, they let him head home and returned to their own room. Before going their separate ways Carly offered him their room's phone number in case anything else struck him in the night, but the three of them agreed to meet at least once more so he would tell them about the book.

"So, what do you think?" Ridley asked Carly as they settled in for bed.

"I think Skip misses his friends," she said sadly. "I think he's the one of that group who actually gave a damn, and he's the one who isn't dead or a bad guy. Has to be a lonely way to live."

Ridley nodded his agreement and turned in.

Chapter 14

Skip settled down by the fire he had stoked earlier. He was in his pajamas and robe, and had just poured himself a man-sized glass of brandy. The thick syrupy alcohol coated his tongue as he drank it and warmed his chest against the year-round cold and damp of the English countryside. He had pulled a book from the shelf at random and was about three chapters into *20,000 Leagues Under the Sea* when the knock on the door came.

He smiled. He knew exactly who it was. Exactly why they'd come. He placed his glass on the side table and gently pulled open the drawer, revealing the Walther PPK inside. He picked up the small gun and placed it, gingerly, into his pocket before standing, readjusting his robe and ambling toward the door.

The knock came again, just as approached.

"Yes, yes. I'm coming."

He opened the door, revealing Nikolas Burns, who was standing on the stoop, looking up and admiring the house.

"You have grown impatient in your old age," Skip said.

Burns smiled back at his old friend.

"Probably. But, you look like hell."

Skip just motioned for him to enter, and headed back toward the parlor.

"You have been skipping your cocktail," Burns said as he stepped in and closed the door behind him. It was a statement, not a question.

"Just cutting back," Skip replied, already retaking his seat. "I figured I would spread it out a bit. It will not last forever, you know."

"Neither will you," said Burns. "Neither will any of us."

Skip retook his seat and his brandy along with it.

"Are you going to offer me one?" Burns asked pointing to the glass.

"You are quite welcome to it. The sideboard is just over there," Skip said with a gesture.

Burns hesitated for a moment, unsure if he wanted to turn his back on his old friend, but relented. He was fairly certain he would be faster. If it were to come to that.

He sauntered over and poured himself a glass, eyeing Skip's collection all the way. Skip, for his part, kept his eyes on Burns's back. Never once breaking his gaze, even as he sipped from his own glass. His hand gripped the pistol in his pocket.

"You've come a long way," Skip finally said. "And all without your toy soldiers."

Burns smiled and raised his glass to Skip in faux ceremony. Skip returned the gesture and they both drank.

"Our toy soldiers," said Burns.

"Not anymore," spat Skip.

"Oh? Then I can stop sending you your checks then?" Burns asked with a curl of his lips. "You may have decided to keep your hands a little less bloody, but do not go convincing yourself that they are, by any means, clean."

"I have no illusions," Skip replied.

Burns smiled back and made his way to the fireplace. "I take it you got my note."

"I did," said Skip. "I feel it best if I waste neither of our time asking the intricacies of how, or who you paid for delivery. But, I will ask why. What do you owe me? Or rather, what do I owe you?"

Burns broke with his pretense of a friendly visit. Time for brass tacks and all that came with them.

"They have the book," he said plainly.

"From their questions, I surmised as much," said Skip.

"Questions?" Burns asked, poorly hiding his nervousness.

"You did not assume they came all this way for my company, did you? Of course they have questions."

"What did you tell them?" Burns swirled the brandy in his glass and did his best to look nonchalant.

"Nothing of merit," Skip said dismissively. "I take it they got it from Ponsley in Tangier. That was what they asked about mostly. Our time with Ponsley. Back when we were young, fresh-faced, boys."

"Back when we were fools," Burns laughed. He sipped the brandy, tasted it, then asked, "Is this the bottle from...."

"Montague's villa? Yes. Well spotted. I assumed you would be coming and opened it special."

"Good man," Burns smiled. "You are nothing if not a

host. WC?"

Skip gestured with his glass.

"End of the hall."

He stood and followed Burns as he crossed the room, and all the way down the little door at the hall's end. There was a pane of frosted glass in it.

"Leave the door open," Skip said, just as Burns went to close it.

"You always were one to watch. You old poof."

Burns turned his back to Skip and lowered his fly, proceeding to do what nature intended of him.

"You know, you should be out there with me. Not here. Rotting away. In fucking Polperro. I once watched you strangle a bloody Somali warlord with those hands of yours. I know you. I would wager, I am the only one who does. Anymore, that is."

As Burns spoke, Skip reached down to the hall table at his side. He didn't need to look, and as such never broke eye contact with Burns's broad back. An old rotary phone sat there. He lifted the receiver, placing it on the table beside him, and proceeded to dial the number he had already committed to memory.

The sound of a flush came, and Burns zipped up his fly. He turned around to face his old friend, and revealed the derringer in his hand. He took a sip from his glass of brandy and said, with a smile, "Now, Old chap. What do you say we get down to business?"

-

The phone rang at some ungodly hour and Ridley cursed it in his bleary, half-conscious state, rolling over to find it. For a brief moment his hand went to reflexively forward the call to voicemail, but stopped when he remembered Skip.

"Hello?" he said, still trying to process the waking world.

On the other end he could hear two voices. They were quiet. Far away.

"Hello?" he said again. No answer.

He was just about ready to hang up, assuming it was a pocket dial, but stopped again when he caught the words the voices were saying, and recognized the voices themselves.

"How much do they know?" That voice was instantly recognizable as the one that had recently started to haunt him in the quiet moments. Those times when things almost seemed normal. Carly and he would be resting or looking at one another with mushy eyes and he would hear it from behind. A gravelly whisper. Burns.

The voice that responded was Skip. "Not much. No more than you would guess. No more than I told them."

There was a pause and Ridley imagined Burns mulling this. "And how much is that? Do they know about Zerzura?"

That word again. It hung in the air. It was so familiar, yet undeniably foreign. Had he heard it before?

He spared a fleeting glance toward Carly, who was still deep asleep, but his attention snapped back to the phone at the sound of the gunshot. Loud and clear, followed by the scrabbling and gurgling sounds of a man fighting vainly in his final moments. Another shot and the other sounds stopped. Just a ragged breath and a few footsteps before the door was opened and closed.

Another sound followed. A scraping sound of something heavy being dragged. Then he heard him loud and clear.

"Are you there?" asked Skip. His voice was ragged and desperate.

Ridley had no idea what to do. Frozen in panic. They had lead Burns here. To Skip.

"He's coming for you. Run."

He immediately dropped the phone and rolled over to shake Carly awake.

"What…what's wrong? What's going on?" she asked.

"We need to leave."

-

It was around four o'clock in the morning when they had finished their frantic and hurried packing and slowly opened the inn's creaking door. The street was completely empty and mostly lit by the moon. The only sounds to speak of were the ocean, the creaking of the gently rocking fishing boats in the bay, and a stray cat out for a nocturnal stroll.

Ridley gestured for Carly to wait before slowly stepping out into the street. He had no idea why the bravery to take the lead had suddenly struck him, but it just as quickly retreated once he was outside. He had never felt more exposed in his life. Carly was no more than two feet behind him, but could easily have been miles away. He was a free-floating beacon in the vacuum of the night. He glanced around, scanning the shadowed cobblestones and quaint little buildings for any sign of impending death. Nothing. He gestured to Carly and the two of them walked out of town wrapped in the eerie silence.

-

On the train back to London, Ridley told Carly in depth about what he had heard. Previously he had only had the chance to give her the bullet points. Skip was dead. Burns killed him and they were clearly next. She took it well.

"So, we know what this is about now," She said digging out the journal.

"I guess we do," he said.

He had sprung for the sleeper car again, more in aid of privacy than sleeping. They were wired in the way that only direct threats can do.

"We could just destroy it," he said, gesturing to the book. Carly had begun to thumb through it. "We destroy it and just go on about our lives. He needs the book. Not us."

"I can't shake the feeling Nick knew something was up," Carly said without looking up from the page. "He died with it in his lap. It's like he saw this all coming."

"One last adventure," he said.

"Maybe he wanted this one to be yours," Carly offered.

She put the book on the table between them, opened to the page with the map. There in Rommel's script, not far south of an unnamed city, was the word Zerzura.

In an instant it flooded back to him.

"I know what Zerzura is."

"You do?" she asked.

"Remember I said it sounded familiar?"

"Yeah." She waited, incredulous, as Ridley scrutinized the map.

"Damn."

"What is it?" she asked.

"We're going to need a pilot."

Chapter 15

Ridley had done a fair amount of research in writing his novels. In fact, it had been remarked upon by a few reviewers over the years. As with any topic, there were always the bits of information one clings to as vital and permanent, and those you let slip by. The third kind is that special sort you squirrel away with perceived intent, but never realize it as other things tend to get in the way. While writing his third novel, "Rex Morgan and the City of Dawn," he had found himself neck-deep in forgotten lore of lost cities around the world. For his fictional city he had drawn inspiration from places like Thuul, or Colonel Fawcett's "Z". But, Zerzera was a whole other animal.

Here is what he knew.

In 1969, reporter and artist Emil Schumacher, while traveling the Middle East, came across the account of a man who had been pulled from the desert outside Benghazi, sometime in the mid-fourteen hundreds. That man told his tale, beginning with the fact that he had been one of several in a caravan, traversing the Sahara.

The caravan ran into trouble when they found themselves in the direct path of a massive sand storm. They did their best to weather it, but as most sand storms tend to last a few hours to a day, this blistering behemoth carried on for a solid week. A week of air too thick with dirt to breathe. Air that shredded any skin left exposed. A week of death for the members of the caravan.

When the storm finally cleared, Hamid Keila was the only one to have survived it. He would go on to wander the desert alone for days. The blistering sun baking his skin. Searing his eyes. He finally fell to exhaustion and dehydration. Half mad from the illusions a deprived mind conjures from the mirages heat plays on sand. It was then, he says, that he was rescued.

Great warriors pulled him from the sands. They fed him and gave him water until his stomach was fit to burst before helping him onto a giant horse. They rode on into a valley between two mountains and it was there that Keila first saw it. A city of pure white. Zerzura.

The streets were filled with women and children bathing in fountains. He knew they couldn't be Muslim, as the
208

women's heads were unveiled, and Keila averted his gaze in disgust. He was taken before these people's king and queen. They showed him great hospitality and continued to feed and clothe him with only the finest. Keila didn't know what to make of the unknown city of riches, where women were uncovered and he heard no calls to prayer. He was a Muslim in a strange land.

-

Sometime later, Hamid Keila would be found stumbling out of the desert, before the gates of Benghazi. Again, he was taken to the highest halls. This time, to the Emir of Benghazi. He told the Emir the whole story from the sandstorm to the fine riches of Zerzura, but when asked why he left the city, he grew cagey. He refused to speak any further and was eventually imprisoned.

They searched him and found a single gold and ruby ring.

-

"Hamid Keila vanishes after that," Ridley continued, leaning against the wall of the compartment. "There are some vague suggestions but, nothing concrete."

"So, where's the ring?" Carly asked.

"It ended up being passed on down the line, eventually inherited by Libya's King Idris. Rumor has it Muammar Gaddafi had it for a time in the Museum of Benghazi, but it vanished in the fall back in two thousand eleven. Researchers were able to determine it was twelfth century European in origin. But, in all the chaos of the Arab Spring, the museum was robbed. No sign or clues to go on."

"Well, seems like we've got a little more than that." said Carly, as she flipped through the book. "Benghazi, huh? Nothing historically bad ever happens there. Looks like you're right. We're going to need a pilot."

-

Ridley had a pilot in mind. It was just a matter of convincing him to fly into what frequently vacillated between a war zone and a post-war zone.

When he found Philippe, it was in Paris and he was

in the midst of every European man's favorite pastime: his ass parked firmly on a bar stool and screaming at the football match. His too-tall body gave his perch a vaguely gargoyle-esque presence. He let out a string of French words Ridley had never learned from Rosetta Stone, and turned for his beer. Realizing it was empty, he flagged down the barman and pointed to his glass.

"I've got this one," Ridley said.

Philippe turned to him, artfully maintaining the long column of ash that clung to the cigarette resting at his mouth's corner. Somewhat bewildered, but appreciative, he nodded.

"You're alive," he said.

"Yeah. But, it's getting harder to maintain," Ridley shot back.

Philippe laughed. "This is called life."

The barman placed two beers in front of them and Ridley shoved some cash at him for them. Philippe lifted his, tipped it to his benefactor, and took a deep sip, turning back to the game.

"I did not expect to see you again," he continued. "Most of the people I fly tend to not want to be seen."

"I have a job for you."

"Oh?"

"And the money's good," Ridley continued.

"Is it dangerous?" he asked, downing his beer and flagging down the barman for another.

"The money's good," Ridley repeated, gesturing to the barman to make it two, and peeling off a couple more bills.

There was a pause as Philippe eyed him with suspicion. The rest of the bar roared at the game, but Philippe never took his eyes off the man with the money. The barman returned with their beers and Ridley noticed for the first time the tattoo on his forearm. Ex-military. Seemed like most of Paris was either ex or current these days.

"Where?" Philippe finally asked.

"Benghazi," Ridley said without hesitation.

The barman reacted and just walked away, not wanting to know where their conversation was headed.

Philippe lowered his eyes, focusing on his beer and tracing his fingers along the condensation, clearly in thought.

"The money's good," Ridley said again.

Philippe snatched up his beer glass and raised it to him. Ridley followed suit.

"Fuck it," said Philippe. "Let's go to Benghazi."

-

When Ridley found Carly in the shitty, fleabag hotel they had checked into upon arrival, she was on her sat phone.

"You can do that?" she asked the person on the other end of the line. "That's great. We're heading out of here in…," She turned to Ridley and he held up four fingers. "Four hours."

While she spoke, he set to work grabbing his stuff, unsure why he even still bothered to unpack at this point.

"Great. We'll see you then," Carly hung up. "So I take it you spoke."

"We did," said Ridley. "And while it serves our purpose, I'm mildly concerned by how little convincing it took."

"Really? We're in full on beggars/choosers territory here. If a no-questions-asked pilot doesn't ask questions, don't question it."

Her logic was pretty solid, if not circular.

"That was Santino," she said.

213

"And?"

"We should be all set. He's getting us press credentials and landing papers."

Santino was one of Carly's contacts from back in her embed days. Social justice-minded thrill seekers. Most of them weren't even affiliated with a specific news source. They were just guys and girls with cameras and backpacks full of the few things they needed or couldn't bear to part with.

It takes a special kind of person to run toward an explosion, or the unmistakable sound of gunfire. But, it's a whole other breed that does so with a camera in hand instead of a gun. Carly had been one once, and Ridley chalked that as another tally toward her comparatively unflappable nature. After losing her husband, she had left that work in favor of the milder, world beauty angle, but still maintained the contacts. Ridley guessed everyone has a quota of the human carnage they can take in a single stretch.

"So, we're really doing this?" he said. More of a statement rather than a question. "We're flying into a recovering war zone to search for lost treasure."

"A charmed life we lead."

Chapter 16

From Paris they flew south over land to Saint-Tropez, and hugged the coast heading east. They bounced along over Cannes, Nice, and Monaco, crossed into Italy, and flew low over Genoa and the pretty painted buildings of Cinque Terre, before cutting south to island hop Corse, Sardegna, and Sicily.

They stayed the night in Malta before going any further. After spending the better part of the previous few days compressed into a space the size of a Volkswagen, and sleeping in whatever hourly hotel they could find near the airfields, it occurred to Ridley that Malta would be their last opportunity to have a good night's sleep in a good bed. Once in Libya, they would be strangers in a strange land, and it was the one place that Burns would be sure to know they were going.

They slept as well as they could that night, Carly and Ridley too tired and nervous to do anything other than hold one another in the overstuffed bed of the suite Ridley had put on his credit card. He had given the last of his hard cash to Philippe as payment and to buy their supplies and fuel. It was official. They were all in on this.

It was with all of this trepidation and uncertainty that they flew into Libyan airspace. They would need to land in Tripoli before, again, coast hopping their way to Benghazi. It was necessity. A string of Arabic came over the static-riddled radio signal. Philippe looked to the both of them. He had no idea what to say to Air Traffic control, a thought that had somehow escaped them. Ridley shrugged.

"Really?" Carly asked, looking to the both of them. She signed and grabbed a headset. "You'd both be lost without me."

She gave them everything they needed, including their (phony) landing credentials. There was a pause as they waited to see if her old buddy Santino really held as much sway as he had promised.

Another string of Arabic crackled over the line and Carly visibly relaxed, prying her fingers from Ridley's seat back. She spoke back to them and the three of them shared a note of celebration.

No anti-aircraft fire.

She was right. They would be lost without her.

They touched down at a small field outside of Benghazi. Carly and Ridley went into town, trusting Philippe to refuel while they were gone. There was no doubt that he could or would. The trust came in form of their belief that he wouldn't take off without them. The honor of a fly-by-night pilot was not beyond repute, but any man willing to fly into this much trouble deserved a modicum of consideration. It should also be mentioned that they had grown quite close over the previous few days. Not only was the plane cramped, but they had run out of wine somewhere over France.

There wasn't much time to spare. Just go to the museum, find out all they could, and head out. There was just enough money for one more night in a hotel. If they needed to be here for more than a day, they would be sleeping in the plane: a prospect none of them looked forward to with great anticipation.

-

Benghazi's Bait-al Medina al-Thaqafi Museum was a classical Ottoman building: covered in balconies, littered with arches, and crowned with a beautiful courtyard fountain. It had once been the home of Omar Pasha Mansour El Kikhia. It rose up before Ridley and Carly, glistening and white as they waded through the sea of street vendors and people making their comings and goings.

They had stopped off on the way for some lamb tajine, courtesy of Carly, and so Ridley now faced the next hurdle of his destiny with a full belly and the memory of orgasmic flavor nipping at the back of his tongue. It was a comfort. More people should face destiny with a full belly than do. (It should be noted that while occasionally glossed over, Ridley was keenly aware of the luck that bore him through all of this. That bore him through his life as a whole. Luck, plain and simple.)

-

Ridley and Carly made their way through the museum's startlingly modern exhibitory. The most haunting of which may have been a recent addition by a sculptor who rendered his works from the discarded weaponry and shell casings that had so recently become commonplace in his world. It was beauty shining through. Like the lamb tajine, it was a subtle, but firm, assertion that these people would endure regardless of what threatened to tear them down. In the end of everything, there will be people and art, and the end will be glorious.

Once they had found the more historically oriented part of the museum, Ridley flagged down a docent.

"Excuse me," he said, doing his best to sound like a befuddled tourist who had chosen his vacation destination anachronistically, "A friend of mine was telling me a story recently. Something about a…lost city. What did he call it?"

He looked to Carly in an attempt to sell his act.

"Zerzura!" he said finally. "He called it Zerzura. Is there anything about that here? Or is it like Atlantis and no one really knows if it's real or not?"

There was a brief moment where the young lady stared at him. From her name tag, he knew her name was Meena.

Carly stepped in and, again, saved the day, repeating everything he had said, sans befuddlement, in Arabic. The two off them spoke rapidly, laughing at what Ridley could only assume was his expense. Meena lead them to a portion of the museum that was less crowded. It was full of roughhewn stone ruins that had been transferred there over the years from various dig sites.

She specifically pointed to a massive gateway carved in stone. Its pediment was adorned with a large, vicious-looking phoenix. More importantly, on a small pedestal in front of the gate was an exact copy of the ring.

Meena went on her museum spiel, which Carly then, in turn, translated for Ridley.

"There is so much we don't know about Zerzera," she said. "This gate is a reconstruction based on testimony found in the Kitab al Kanuz. The ring is actually one found by the only person believed to have ever seen Zerzura. A man by the name of Hamid Keila. He came out of the desert and presented this ring to the Emir of Benghazi as a trophy of his time in the mysterious white city."

As she spoke, Ridley tried to take in every detail of what was said and what he saw. The gate was gargantuan. It was strange, though. Aside from the rather menacing-looking flaming bird crowning the pediment, there was no other adornment. There weren't even doors. As gates to mysterious lost cities go, it seemed strangely lacking.

"Ask her where we can get a copy of the Kitab al Kanuz," Ridley said to Carly.

The two women exchanged a quick couplet before Carly emerged with a simple answer.

"It vanished."

-

Ridley and Carly found Philippe at a small cafe and joined him for a coffee. He briefly acknowledged their arrival, but his attention was focused on the televised football match. They were a few behind, but had no intention of catching up.

"Well that was a bust," said Ridley.

"Maybe," replied Carly, reaching over to plunge a hand into his bag and pulling out the book.

"An idea?"

"No." She shrugged. "But, as a writer I expect you should respect the value of A: research, and B: making a back-up."

As she spoke, she pulled a notebook from her own bag and a pencil from under her head scarf, and began to copy the final pages and map from the book. It was broad strokes, the general idea, rather than a perfect representation.

The waiter came around.

"Hal 'ahdar lak shayyana akhr?" he asked.

Ridley looked to each of them, and after a series of nods, ordered them another round.

"So, what do we do now?" he asked as the waiter walked off to fill their order. "This next round represents the last of our cash."

"Excuse me," said a man at the next table. "Are you an American?"

"Well, that depends on a number of factors," retorted Ridley.

"That's fair." The man laughed and extended a hand. "Victor Laughlin. I'm just trying to find a good place to spend the night around here."

Ridley reached out to shake Victor's hand, noting his own reflection in the man's gold-rimmed, round sunglasses, but just then a crowd of children rushed their table. Given that they weren't ordering food, whatever they were saying was outside of Ridley's Arabic vocabulary. But, their tiny grasping hands and practiced sad expressions gave context. They were hungry. Carly smiled and handed them each a piece of flatbread. They thanked her and ran off.

"Now where were we?" asked Ridley, turning back to Victor. But, Victor wasn't there. "Okay. That's weird."

"Oh, my God. Ridley."

He spun in his chair to see what was wrong, and saw that Carly was already on her feet.

"The book is gone!"

"Oh, shit," said Ridley. They both glanced around. "You take the kids. I'll find Charley."

She nodded and bolted after them. Ridley looked to Philippe, who just raised his class in a cheers.

"Bon voyage," said the Frenchman.

-

Ridley ran through the crowded streets, looking for any sign of the man who may or may not have been Victor Laughlin. He had only seen him in that quick glance. Was he blonde? Maybe. Tall? Short? Who knew?

"Son of a bitch."

There! Two blocks up he saw him. Those same round sun glasses were scanning the crowd, and Ridley ducked into an alley to avoid them. After a moment, he peaked out and saw Victor heading away rapidly.

225

He plunked down a few coins at a stand and grabbed a shemagh scarf, wrapping it around his head to cover all but his eyes, and made his way quickly through the crowd. He gained on Victor quickly. The book was in plain sight, tucked haphazardly under his left arm.

He was close. Ten feet at the most, and gaining. Ridley stretched out his hand. His fingers just barely grazed the book's edge.

-

Carly could see the group of children ahead of her. They had finished their flat bread and were hassling another group of tourists.

"Ugh. This is ridiculous."

She turned and headed back to the restaurant.

-

Victor turned suddenly to see Ridley and his

outstretched hand, and immediately punched him in the face.

He hit the ground as Victor took off running.

"Okay," said Ridley, shaking his head and waiting for his vision to clear. "I guess subtlety's out."

In an instant he was on his feet and moving deftly through the crowd at a sprint. He and Victor tore through the streets, ducking around carts, leaping trashcans, and narrowly missing being hit by cars.

Victor ducked into a doorway, and Ridley had to slide to stop in time to follow him. It was a hotel, and Victor took hold of a cart full of luggage from a busboy, throwing it in Ridley's direction. He reacted quickly. Catching the cart, he kicked the luggage off and climbed aboard, kick-pushing to get up to speed.

Victor ran, shoving hotel guests and staff out of his way and as they regained their composure. They were forced to dodge the high-speed, oncoming Ridley.

Victor came to the end of the hall. It ended at the mezzanine of the hotel pool, and he ran for the staircase down. Ridley saw the railing dead ahead, and took the gamble, speeding up rather than slowing down. When the cart hit, the momentum transferred and Ridley was launched through the air. As he came down, he grabbed hold of Victor and the two of them landed in the pool. They fought, struggling and sinking, as the hotel patrons vacated, some screaming.

Victor grabbed Ridley by the throat and squeezed. Ridley fought as hard as he could, struggling to land punches that were slowed by the water. But, he could feel his strength starting to slip away. He was tired. Eventually, the pain subsided. In the end, it became easier to just let go.

Once his work was done Victor climbed out and grabbed a towel someone had abandoned. He picked up the book from where it had landed at the pool's edge and walked off.

-

It was quiet for a while. Haunting. Lonely. He floated there. Weightless. Between life and death. Was this what it all added up to? He hadn't seen his family in years. Now he never again would. He thought of his nieces and nephews. Thought of what his sister and brother might tell them about where their uncle Ridley had gone. How that story might change as they got older and slightly more able to handle the truth. Somehow, he didn't think they would start with, "He was drowned to death in a hotel pool in Benghazi, Libya by a man he had never met."

He pondered the darkness that extended before him. This was it. This was all any of us would be. All we are. He was okay with it.

-

Something broke the water's surface with a hard splash. It moved gracefully and took hold of him, lifting and pushing him to the surface. Together they broke through and moved to the pool's edge.

With a great effort Philippe climbed out and pulled Ridley after him. He rolled him over and started chest compressions and mouth-to-mouth. He kept it on. Again and again. No response. Again. Still nothing. Philippe wouldn't stop. Among other reasons, this man still owed him money.

With a cough, a sputter, and a hack, Ridley clawed his way back to life. Philippe turned him to his side and let the fluid clear from his lungs.

Once he could finally speak again, Ridley turned to his savior.

"Merci beaucoup."

Philippe shrugged. "De rien."

He placed a cigarette to his lips and went to light it before realizing that it, like everything else on him, was waterlogged.

-

The man who, at least for today, went by Victor Laughlin, arrived at the pre-agreed upon meeting point. He had made a career of being other people. He could be whomever you needed if the money was right. A prince on more than one occasion. A playboy more often than not. He spoke more than ten languages, knew fifteen different fighting styles, and had contacts with similar skills in every major city and squirrelly foxhole the world over.

Today he was hired to play the tourist. Tomorrow he had a meeting in Qatar. But, first there was business to attend to. He would hand over the book, accept his comically large payment, and be off to play the part of a noble woman's consort in just a few hours.

He bellied up to the rooftop bar and, with a wry smile, ordered a Vesper martini. Two measures of gin, one of vodka, half of lilet blanc, served ice cold in a champagne coup with a twist of lemon. It was strong and terrible, but as its inventor had said, "All terrible things should be taken in large doses."

Officially, alcohol was illegal in Libya. A nationwide prohibition for the sake of religious purity. But, like anywhere else, if you knew the right people, ran in the right circles, and were flush with cash, you could find that such laws were enforced for the plebeians only. As the bartender placed the perfectly-poured drink in front of him, he heard footsteps at his back.

"Better make that two." said a gravelly, English-accented voice.

A second drink was poured in record time, and the two men found themselves a nice secluded corner table, where they could speak privately while several members of Pandora Dawn did their best to appear as inconspicuous bar goers.

"I believe this is what you were after," said Victor, producing the book and sliding it across the table.

His guest took a long sip of martini. "Did you look at it?"

"Do you have my money?"

The Englishman smiled and, with a snap of his fingers, a man appeared at his side with a silver Zero Haliburton briefcase. This man placed the case in front of Victor and disappeared into the crowd of regular bar patrons.

Victor opened the case, picked a stack of cash at random, and flipped through the bills. Satisfied by their authenticity, he closed the case again and stood.

"When you pay double my asking price, you pay me not to pry. Am I curious? Of course. But, I recognize that people with your kind of funding, aside from generally not being the sort to trifle with, are more valuable as return customers."

With that, he stood, downed the last of his martini and said, "Do look me up next time you need...well, anything. The Network appreciates your business, Sir." He turned to leave.

"Give my regards to Veronica," said the Englishman.

"But of course." And with a smile, Victor Laughlin was gone, and the man who had been him disappeared into the crowd.

Chapter 17

"I'm just glad you're alive," said Carly, once Ridley had recounted to her what had happened.

He and Philippe met her at their hotel and, after bemoaning Libya's prohibition on alcohol, the three of them began to assemble a plan of what to do next.

"I think it's safe to assume that 'Victor,' whoever he was, was working for Burns," said Ridley.

"Clearly," replied Carly. "So, now that he has the book, are we off the hook? Does this mean we can go home now?"

"I doubt it. We know too much. What are the chances an army of mercenaries are just going to let us walk away?" asked Ridley. "The upside is they think I'm dead. I mean, if you can call that an upside. So, in the end it's really up to you. But, we've come this far. We have the pages you copied. The map. Why don't we just…go?"

Carly considered it for a while. She pulled the pages from her bag and unfolded them, laying them out on the hotel table in front of her.

"Do we do this?" she asked.

"I'm not going to ask you to," said Ridley. "It's your choice. I know you've lost a lot, and I'm not going to make you do this."

"If we do," Carly said, after a moment, "and I'm not saying yes. We'll be racing an army of mercenaries to a mythical lost city, with nothing but a few scattered pages and four-seater plane."

They both looked to Philippe who had, till now, sat quietly by the window, ignoring the hotel's no smoking policy.

"We're not going to force you to either," said Ridley.

The Frenchman put out his cigarette in his coffee cup. "I do not want you to misunderstand. I came for the money. But, by now, I would consider us…not friends. How do you say…. Aussi proche qu'un frère."

This struck Ridley. "Thank you."

Philippe lit another cigarette. "I am in."

236

Carly took a deep breath and stood up. "Me, too."

"Okay," said Ridley. "Let's go do something stupid."

-

It was still dark when they boarded Philippe's plane one more time. Among the three of them there wasn't a single sarcastic joke to be made. The gravity of what they were about to do hung over them. They all knew that they were flying into the desert with the vaguest shadow of a plan, in search of something that may not be there.

Carly and Philippe were there for him. But, Ridley was there for Nick. For everything Nick had been. For everything Nick had represented to him. For the last great adventure.

They flew on in darkness for the better part of an hour before the sun began to crest the dunes. As it came up, the light washed over the sea of glittering gold that was the Sahara and they could see that for miles in every direction there was nothing. They kept going.

"We have another hour before we will have to turn back. But, I can lean the fuel mixture out," said Philippe. "Get us another forty-five minute reserve if we fly at our highest."

237

"Do what you have to," said Ridley.

Philippe nodded, flipped a few switches, and pulled back on the yoke, taking the plane higher. The dunes below began to blend into a single sheet of gold. They kept going.

As they neared the PNR (point of no return) Philippe looked to his two charges. They were asleep. He reached a hand over to rouse Ridley, but stayed it before making contact. Something else caught his eye. Something in the distance. At first it was a spark on the horizon. Philippe looked at his fuel gage, weighed what he had to work with, and opted to investigate. They had come this far.

Philippe turned a few degrees west until the spark was dead on. Only in the few seconds it had taken to make the adjustment, it had gone from a spark to a flame, and continued to grow. It was a conflagration. It was a second sun, rising between two mountains.

The dancing light stirred Ridley, and as he opened his eyes, he struggled at first to contextualize what he was seeing.

"My god." He looked to Philippe who only broke eye contact with the unnatural fire to pencil quick notes on his knee mounted clipboard of charts. "Carly!"

Lying in the back seat of the plane, she, too, struggled to wake up, but when she did, she was just as mystified. She placed a hand on Ridley's shoulder, leaning in to get a better view.

The blazing light was now large and clearly a free-standing structure, nestled at the far end of a valley. The desert stretched on beyond it. The peaks of towers began to be discernible just when the anti-aircraft fire began.

"Hang on!" Philippe shouted. He tilted the yoke forward and worked the pedals, bringing them hard around to the left, trying frantically to turn them back. The air exploded around them. Rapid fire blasts of flames and smoke appeared and clung to the sky with concussive force, and the Frenchman was forced to fly evasively.

The shot that took their wing off sucked the air out of the world. Ridley lost all sense of sound and time. He felt that same loss of panic and pain he had experienced at the bottom of that hotel pool. He looked at Philippe, who still frantically pulled at the yoke and worked the pedals in a stubborn refusal to acknowledge his powerlessness in his final moments.

Ridley looked to Carly. She was panicked. She was saying something, but he couldn't hear her. Their eyes locked. He didn't need to hear her. He didn't even need to read her lips.

"I love you," she said.

There was nothing else. There was no time. There was

only fire.

-

Ridley woke up, his senses too overwhelmed with sensation for his mind to sort through at first. There was heat. A lot of it. Too much of it. A heavy smell of oil and smoke filled his nostrils. Burning. Something was burning. That much was clear. Judging by the crackling and the pinging sounds of expanding metal all around, he began to suspect it was a fire. A large one. One of which he was clearly at the center.

His body ached. All of it. Too much to move. Too much to even open his eyes. Nothing felt broken, but he still knew he did not have the ability to climb out from under the wreck. This, he thought, with no small amount of Byronic romance, was how he would die. Alone, confused, and in rapidly increasing pain.

There was a pressure under his arm. No. It was under both arms. Suddenly, with a jostle and sharp tug, he could feel the heat begin to recede. He was being pulled. He just managed to open his eyes, but they couldn't focus, and his savior's face was obscured further by the sun, which at this moment rimmed their head like a halo.

They dropped him. It was unceremonious and painful, and his fall was only barely cushioned by the searing sand he landed on. There was another thump to his left, which after some intense effort, he rolled over to find was a badly burned Philippe. The skin of his right side had peeled away with the material of his shirt. Ridley's pain did not seem nearly as bad. As he looked ahead, he could see another man dragging Carly away from the plane.

The plane. He could see it now. Though, it was barely recognizable to look at. He could piece together what had happened. The one remaining wing was some distance behind the main wreck. It lay where it had been torn off as the plane cartwheeled and bounced along the dunes. The tail was in pieces, leaving the cockpit as a flaming extension from a ragged nothing.

Looking around, it became abundantly clear that the heavily armed men of Pandora Haze surrounded them.

"Give them room." said a strong, gravelly voice. "Let them breath."

The wall of mercenaries parted, and a tall, grave-looking old man dressed in gabardine trudged up the dune, coming to a rest just above Ridley's head. He crouched.

"We have quite a bit to talk about."

Skip looked good for his age.

-

"You are probably a mite curious as to the nature of my survival," said Skip.

He was gazing out the window of a finely appointed tent. One of those multi-room affairs. There were tables cluttered with maps and old books, and a bar that held Scotch and Port in abundance.

Ridley strained against the ropes that bound his wrists to the bamboo chair's back.

"Nicolas and I started Pandora Haze together. All those years ago." There was a mournful reflection in his voice. "It has always been about Zerzera. The mercenaries, the library in Thrace, all of it was for this." He turned to face Ridley, the journal open in his hands to the photograph of he, Burns, and Ponsley.

"I never wanted to cut Ponsley out. That was all Nicky's doing."

"Why are you telling me this?" Ridley piped up with
equal parts curiosity and confusion.

Skip seemed genuinely surprised, as if he had forgotten from whom he was receiving confessional.

"A number of reasons. First of which is that I find it important to illustrate the hard truths of democracy in action and dispel any hard won illusions. You see, the man with more money, more power, and more guns also, transitively, holds more votes."

Ridley could not, in good faith, argue with this.

"Secondly, I would say that it is important to me that any word of this not be taken under false prejudice."

Skip gestured and Ridley looked around to see two men he had not noticed before. They moved on him and, for a moment, Ridley strained against his bounds, ready to fight whatever they came to deal. One of the men flicked open a butterfly knife with a practiced gesture, and with a quick and deliberate motion, cut Ridley's ropes.

Skip circled around to the tent's entrance, pausing at the flap.

"You are, I would be willing to wager, a bit confused. I cannot blame you. But, allow me to clarify my actions. You see, unlike my colleague, I have no interest in your death."

Ridley stood, rubbing his wrists, and limped toward

Skip. Neither the old man nor his men made moves for their ready weapons. There was no need to. In his current state, Ridley couldn't hurt anyone.

"We are standing on the edge of something glorious here, you and I," said Skip. "Something glorious."

With a flourish, Skip threw back the flap of the tent, and for the first time, Ridley laid eyes on it.

Zerzura.

-

It is impossible to explain the brilliance of the city. It would be just as easy an effort to explain sight to the blind, or an unseen color to those without the range to perceive it. But, linger not in imagined notions. What can be told is that directly before the camp, some two hundred yards ahead, stood an archway of the whitest marble. It was the only part cleanly visible. The city beyond stretched high above it and caught the sun so perfectly as to shine with a brilliance that may lead one to think they were in the presence of two such heavenly lights.

This arch, like the one in the museum in Benghazi, was crowned with a pediment that depicted a phoenix in mid-rise.

To either side of it, gargantuan statues knelt, carved of the darkest black ebony. Were they to stand, each of them would tower at forty feet with ease.

Skip stepped forward and, through a megaphone, blasted out a call to order.

"Okay, now. Send another!"

At the furthest edge of the camp, Ridley could see chaos erupt as several men pushed and shoved one of them toward the arch. He fought and kicked, but the masses won out and he was thrown hard to the sand.

The rest of the crowd backed away, leaving him a lonely island just beyond the camp's domain. This man stood on shaky feet and looked back in vain to the men who had betrayed him. One stepped forward and tossed something to him. A bottle. It landed at his feet and stood upright in the sand. If any of them spoke a word, Ridley couldn't hear it.

Skip stepped to Ridley's side, his own eyes not leaving the lone man.

"We have not, as of yet, been able to circumvent the city's defenses."

The man crouched down, grabbed the bottle, and staggered toward the archway. His hands shook too hard for him to open it, try as he might. In the end, he gave up and pulled the cork out with his teeth. The bottle was at his lips and tilted to the sky as he drank deep, in a knowingly foolish attempt to numb what he knew was coming. What he had seen happen to others before. He drained the bottle and cast it to the sands before continuing to march toward the arch.

For a while nothing happened. The whole camp was so silent that even at this distance, Ridley swore he could hear the shift of the sand under the man's feet. He stopped between the two statues, just shy of the line cast from the noon sun over the arch. He glanced back for a moment, and the look on his face was clearly read as fear and the courage that it took to keep him standing.

He turned back and took the step. It was a moment, but to him and any man who watched, it was an eternity. At first, there was nothing. Then came a rumble that grew to a cacophony. The man stepped back and the rumble stopped. All silent but the wind. He turned to run, but another man was waiting, and fired a round that struck the sand just shy of his feet.

"Not one step back!" bellowed the man with the rifle.

The sacrificial man knew what had to come next. He took a deep breath and took two steps forward. The rumbling began again. It grew and shook the arch and statues. No. Not the arch. Just the statues. And, they were not shaking. They were moving. Rising up to their full height. Towering ebony colossi whose shadows were as black as those that cast them.

A number of things happened now, and in rapid sequence. The man ran. Beyond the arch way was a long corridor that extended into the city. He ran as fast as he could in the sand. It was an arm-pumping, high kneed run that carried him about a quarter of the way before they caught him. The statues moved with surprising speed for their size. Many expect giants to be slow, a false paradigm given to us by the world of cinema. Godzilla moved slowly so as to lend the illusion of massive weight. But, in truth, the massive guardians of Zerzura were fast. Fast enough that the heart of every viewer would drop, had they not already hit rock bottom at their first sight of the golems.

The guardians stepped over the arch without effort, and were on the man in a moment. One slammed its fist down hard in front of him while the other grabbed him by the legs, tossing him high into the air. A massive open hand caught him with a bone shattering slap that drove him back to the ground. Finally, a fist landed hard on what was left of the man. The two statues returned to their watch posts. They had added a fifth to the unrecognizable splotches of red that dotted the sand between them and the camp.

Ridley stood stock still as all of this happened. He was paralyzed by pure shock. There was literally no experience in his life that could have prepared him for this. Granted, there was no experience in his life that could have prepared him for rooftop gunfights. Or a multi-national chase. Or surviving a plane crash, for that matter. It had been a long couple of weeks.

Skip seemed unfazed, lifting the megaphone to his mouth once again. "All right! Cast lots! We go again top of the hour!"

The words were calm but authoritative. His command was unquestionable. Not a man thought twice of his order. One by one the group turned in to look at one another, and again began their process of selection. Velcro name patches were dropped into a boonie hat. The pulled name, spelling death for its owner, was then placed on a cloth band with the others. Other names. Other men. Other brothers. Parsons, Reynolds, Michaels, Forrester, Washburne, and now Baker.

Rather than tears or anger, there came a cheer. And why not? Baker had a whole forty –five minutes left. Another bottle went around. Cheers continued, and they would for the rest of Baker's time. Then he would step forward, the fear slowly descending upon him in much the same manner as his situation's reality. He would step forward as the others had, and maybe, just maybe, learn some trick, or glimpse some flaw in the city's defenses that they had missed. Maybe he would be the one. Maybe he would survive.

At the day's end, the number of name badges below Baker's had swelled. In total, twelve men had died. Each of them thinking the same thing. Maybe them. Nothing had been learned.

"Take him to see his friends," Skip said, and returned to his tent, set on imagining all new means of ingress.

Chapter 18

Ridley was taken, at gun point, to the camp's medical tent. Aside from the few burns suffered pulling the three of them from the wreck, the only injuries sustained by Pandora Dawn on this venture were those not worth bringing to Medical. As such, on this visit, the patients were outnumbered by those assigned to attend to them.

Carly sat upright on her bed, holding an ice pack to her neck. Her forearms were wrapped and bandaged. Small cuts and bruises littered her body, but she didn't look vulnerable or frail in any way. No. She looked pissed off.

"Ridley, thank God," she said without rising. She was happy to see him, but too sore all over to express it. Her eyes watered as a means of portraying both conditions.

"Where's Philippe?" he asked.

Carly stiffly gestured to a curtain, behind which Ridley could see a number of people working, in surgical masks and gloves.

"How bad is he?"

"Pretty bad," Carly answered. "What the hell do we do now?"

She was asking him? She was the one with the tactical knowledge. The field experience. Hell, he had watched her personally end several of these mercenaries. But, she was asking him "what do we do now?" as if he was meant to know.

Ridley thought. He didn't have any of her skills, or history. He had handled a gun at the range as a rebellious teenager. Taken those tang su do lessons as a child. Could any of that apply? Of course not. Who was he kidding to even think it might?

Ridley's only real skills these days amounted to writing, smoking hash, and listening to old men tell stories.

-

"Mind if I come in?" Ridley asked.

The atmosphere was surprisingly lax around the camp. While every mercenary was armed, and there were guards posted at the armory tent, there was an understanding that Ridley and the others were no threat, and as such, didn't really register as security concerns. Sure, in open air they had held their own. Rather, Carly had. But, that was in smaller groups, and urban settings. Too many nagging little hidey-holes. Out here, in the desert, hemmed in by the valley, and with these numbers of mercenaries, it would be foolhardy to even attempt anything. This was why when he approached Skip's tent, there were no guards. Only an open flap, framing the man within bent over a table of books and maps.

Skip's head snapped up at the sound of his voice.

"Ah, Ridley," said the old man, squinting through his glasses. "Come in. Come in. I dare wager I may be able to use your help on this. Extra eyes and all that."

Ridley entered, and calmly strode up to the table, trying equally hard to watch the man, the exits, and see what he was looking at.

"Now. According to Keila's account in the Kitab al Kanuz, There's a key we seem to be missing."

"A key?"

"Yes. Not literal, I should imagine. Things like this tend   253 to be metaphorical, or a cipher of some kind."

"And you think, this key is going to get you past those...things?" Ridley asked.

"Guardians," Skip interjected. "And do not think for one moment you will not be coming with us."

"Why would I?"

Skip laughed to himself.

"You mean aside from the army standing between you and I? I would say because every moment you are by my side is a moment you are still alive. We will be picking up stakes and carrying everything on through with us. No water or scrap of food left behind. So, you are perfectly welcome to stay behind if you like; however, I would draw your attention to two simple facts. The first is that you have hundreds of miles of unbroken, unforgiving desert in every direction. The second? If, until now, no one has ever found this city, what are the chances anyone will ever find you?"

His lips curled into something more sinister than a smile as these words left them.

Unsettled by this plain statement of his circumstances, Ridley looked at the book that Skip was hunched over. It was old. Not just old but ancient. He could tell from the way Skip hovered his fingers just above the pages that they were a shaky hand or gust of wind away from cracking into dust.

"Still no sign or symbol of this key," Skip muttered, mostly to himself.

"Is this it? The Kitab?" Ridley asked incredulously.

Skip smiled and stood up straight, impressing Ridley with his full height.

"Wondering how I got my villainous hands on it, aren't you?" he said, laughing. "Then again, I assume you've learned by now that I am a man with…methods."

Ridley moved his glance quickly to the page.

"How much do you know about it?" Skip asked.

"Not much, honestly. A girl at the museum in Benghazi brought it up, but prior to that I'd never even heard the words."

"Did she take to mentioning its provenance? Where it had come from? Where it might have gone?"

Ridley shook his head.

"Well, I cannot speak for where it came from, or its initial disappearance for that matter, but as for how it got to this table, your friend Ponsley played a hand in the making.

"I tell you this because I believe the time for illusions is

255

over and done. You fought long and hard to be here. The hunt for what's out there is just as much your passion now as any of ours. You have earned the right to know what brought us all this far.

"It was the last job the three of us ever pulled together. The real last job. I presume you have divined the last story was total fantasy by now. There was no cliff top fight, and Burns did not fall to a watery death in a decidedly Sherlockian turn.

"Honestly, had I known he was on you, I would not have included that bit. Though he never tells me anything these days, so there you go. Terrible way to try to run a company, for the record. An amount of independence is important, but partnership requires…communication. Had I known he planned to move on Ponsley and the book, we could have worked it out together. Instead of his sending me a haphazard last minute letter. By then he had bollocksed it to the point of idiocy. I do not have much use for that sort of person. Friend or no.

"Of course, I am going beyond now. I tend to do that these days. Where was I? Ah, yes the book. First filed in the great halls of the Emir himself. The self-same one that grilled our friend Keila after he stumbled out of the desert.

"You see, popular theory is that Hamid Keila himself wrote the Kitab al Kanuz, while imprisoned in Benghazi. Refusing to explain what it was he 'escaped' from in there, the Emir had him banged up for what ended up being life. Somewhere in that time, he is said to have started to write down all he was willing to say about his experiences. A sort of memoir. Turns out the old man was in our line of work. A tomb robber. He included the legends of several other lost treasures and cities. Their traps and curses. Their signs and symbols. All in cryptic rhyme, of course. But, for some reason, on Zerzura he would not budge. Not a word more than he had told them all on that very first day. Something, it would seem, had Keila terrified.

"So, he passes on, as men do, taking with him any secret he had not put down, and the book, after rigorous study, found itself a nice comfy shelf to rest and collect dust on. Ages pass, the shelves change and, eventually, it finds its way to a black market auction in Tuvalu. Those were the sort of circles me and the boys were running with in those days. Men who knew how to get things. A detailed history of ownership not included.

"I was the one to find the listing, you know. Called the boys together and did the heavy planning on how we might free it from the auction's stores before it ever hit the block. That was who we had become by then. You see, any treasure hunter of note–if at it long enough–will develop certain skills. Be it simple bribery of customs officials, or knowing one's way around the aggressive end of negotiations. We were, by then, well-practiced thieves in the night.

"The work itself was not at all difficult. We made it in and out. Not a casualty to speak of on the security staff. No. That was not the hard part. The hard part came when Ponsley decided to turn his back on us. Decades of friendship and brotherhood fell by the wayside as he suddenly suffered an attack of conscience.

"Seems he felt we had strayed too far from the purer faith of antiquity. I cannot say it was an unfounded thought. He had always been in it for the adventure, whereas Burns and I had begun to see the more lucrative end of those new skills I mentioned.

"He was filled with clichés. 'I never signed up for any of this.' Or 'When did it stop being about the search?' But, he was there with us the whole way. Every job we pulled. Every stately home burgled. Every last throat slit. His hands were just as dirty as ours.

"So, what were we to do? We could not just let him to walk away. Not with everything he knew. Of course not. And while I was against taking the more final measures Burns suggested, I saw their merits to be certain. But, it never came to that. It never had the chance to.

"Ponsley, it seems, decided to make his own moves. He stole Rommel's diary and ran."

At this point, Skip pulled the familiar old leather book from his pocket and placed it on the table. He looked on it with a reverence that seemed newly found.

"This little book," he continued. "He knew that without it the Kitab al Kanuz, and all we had done to get hold of it, meant nothing. And as long as he had it, it would not be smart of us to risk crossing him off either. He could easily have hidden it. Taking its location with him to the grave. Distractions came up, as they do–the revolution in Congo if I remember correctly–and what with him having nearly the skill of yours truly, we lost sight of him.

"You see, that blasted kraut had the route all figured. Hitler's funding to his occult division is legendary, and his reach, even in allied land, was great. In fact, I believe that had it not been for our happening upon their camp that night, all those years ago, it is very possible Der Führer would have found the city. Wiping us all away to build his new Reich on our ashes."

Skip stepped away from the table and headed for the tent's flap, beckoning Ridley to follow. He pointed out over the moonlit camp to the city and its dormant guardians.

"Just think. What secrets could those monstrosities be protecting? What ancient mysteries could we solve? In the end, it would seem, of the three of us, I was the most pure. I never gave up on the hunt. The search for truth. I knew Burns had, even when we first decided to start Pandora Dawn, but I went along with it anyway. Because, you see, unlike Ponsley, I recognize that belief is not, and never has been, enough. This world and this life are not for those who halve their measures.

"I taught Burns that lesson back in Polperro."

-

Ridley left Skip's tent feeling disillusioned and angry, and walked to the camp's edge. He was right. There was nowhere to go. Nothing for miles. Just the gently sloping dunes and shadows cast by the moonlight.

This had all been his fault. He saw that now. Clearly. Ponsley had gone into hiding, taking the one name they wouldn't think to look for him under. But, when Ridley wrote the article telling the world that he had died, he practically sent up a signal flare. Burns, without informing his partner, came running. And, the rest was a deadly history.

What would come next? Would they stay here until the systematic loss of life reached the absurd? Who knew just how many bodies Skip had already stepped over to get this far? What difference would a few dozen more make?

From where he stood, something caught Ridley's eye. A shadow out of place. Maybe not a shadow, but something dark where there should only have been light. It wasn't terribly far from the camp's edge, and wouldn't be hard to reach. With nothing better to do, he set off for it.

He had only walked a few hundred yards before the shape came clear. It was what was left of Philippe's plane. A charred and empty shell, cracked and twisted, half buried in sand. Debris was strewn in a rough line of impact direction.

He navigated that field of scorched metal haltingly, watching for anything sharp hidden just below the sand's surface and eventually reached the main fuselage. It was a husk. Completely burned out. Neither the seats nor the instrument panel were recognizable.

Suddenly, a thought occurred to Ridley. Maybe. Just maybe. He reached down into the sand near what he thought may have been the plane's luggage compartment and found the handle. It was stuck shut, but he found a large, flat piece of metal that he wedged into the crack of the opening and pried loose.

A blast of air wafted out, carrying with it the scent of cooked meat. It was his Florentine leather duffle, or rather what was left of it. Now it was just as charred as the rest of the wreckage. Still, it was possible.

He dug a hand inside and fished around. There was a spot where the lining was loose. He had cut and resewn it years ago to make the space between the bag and the lining usable as an extra secret pocket. It was in here that he groped around. It was in here that he found it.

His hand closed on something hard inside of something stiff and flaking. As he pulled it out, the moonlight caught the pile of near ashes in his hand. Barely legible was his name in Nick's handwriting. The wind kicked up and he let it take the layers as he caught the fleeting words left of the letter.

...LET HER KNOW... WASTED LIFE ... LIVE FOR YOU...

As the last piece was carried off in the breeze, all that remained in his hand was a single gold and ruby ring.

-

Ridley walked around the camp's edge, doing his

best to stick in the shadows of the dunes and the cliff side that extended above him. A handful of clouds peppered the otherwise crystalline sky, on a course for the full moon. From where he stood, he could see the Pandora Dawn soldiers as they cut loose around a large bonfire at the camp's center. They drank, laughed, and shared stories of the men they had lost on that day and others long passed.

A few more seconds and he would have the cover of full darkness. The clouds were moving quickly, and he knew just as fast as the darkness came, it would be gone again. He would have to move.

And there it was. The moon was blocked, and its light that fell over the city and the camp was blocked with it. Ridley bolted across the sand, his arms pumping. His feet moved fast enough that they barely had time to sink into the shifting surface.

He crossed the space between the camp and the city gate on an angle, dodging around the crushed and broken corpses of the men Pandora Dawn was busy celebrating. When he finally slowed, breathing heavily and sweating in the cold night air, he stood at the foot of one of the guardians.

It was bigger than he thought, towering at nearly fifty feet while seated. He slowly circled around it. It didn't show any sign of standing. Any sign that it moved at all. It was

263

colossal and stoic. Had he not seen the earlier display, he never would have guessed that it was capable of moving with a startling speed.

Something caught Ridley's attention. A whisper. Possibly several. The direction of its origin was distinct. It came from the long alley that stretched from between the guardians and deep into the city. It was beautiful. Hypnotic. As he turned his attention to the sound, he was transfixed by the image of a beautiful androgynous being. It stood in the middle of the long alley, clothed in white samite that seemed to glow even in the darkness. They beckoned to him, and he followed.

That was when the clouds passed from their place in front of the moon. As the light filtered back down over the landscape, the figure vanished as quickly as they had appeared, and Ridley found himself roughly thirty feet into the city, beyond the guardians. He looked back at them. They were just as still as they had been before.

Something was warm in his pocket. He reached for it and pulled out the ring. The stone was glowing faintly. He turned it over in his hand, before glancing back to where the figure had stood.

"Well, that's interesting."

Chapter 19

Carly was asleep in the medical tent. Rather, she was hovering on that edge of sleep where her thoughts had just begun to drift into the realm of the absurd. This didn't help the circumstances of Ridley's entrance. He crept in, digging under the tent's edge, and slipped up beside her cot.

"Hey."

Carly rolled over, blearily.

"What? Wait. What is…?"

"Shhh. Shhh. It's me."

Her eyes cleared just enough to make him out in the dark.

"What are you doing?" she asked.

"I have a plan on how we're going to get out of here. Where is Philippe?"

She loosely gestured to another cot on the far side of the room. Philippe lay on it, with most of his body covered in bandages. He wore an oxygen mask, and a monitor signaled his steady heartbeat.

Ridley slowly approached him.

"Hey buddy. Est-ce que ça va?"

Philippe opened his eyes and nodded slowly.

"I got you something," Ridley said, reaching into his bag and pulling out a beer.

Philippe smiled.

"I know it's asking a lot, but do you think you could fly if I got you a plane?" Ridley asked.

Philippe pulled the oxygen mask from his face.

"I can always fly."

"Good. These guys have three big cargo planes on the east end of the camp. It's how they got all of this shit out here."

Philippe gripped the side of his cot hard and painfully raised himself to a sitting position. Once upright, he held out his hand. Ridley passed him the beer. Philippe took a long swig from it.

"How do you expect for us to just leave with one of their planes?" asked Carly.

"I have a plan."

-

"This is a terrible plan," Carly said, as they headed out across the sand.

It was late and the entire camp was silent, as everyone had already turned in. There was nothing but the gentle howl of wind in the night, and the whispers between the two of them.

"Well, you're more than welcome to head back," said Ridley. "Or come up with a plan of your own."

The moon had shifted and the shadows were now longer and deeper than they had been earlier, when Ridley had made the same trip alone.

They were nearing the gates. The guardians still stood as stoic as ever.

"So, what makes you so sure we won't be…you know, 'crushed' like these guys?" Carly asked, gesturing to the corpses.

"Because he already has the key," said Skip.

He stepped out of the shadows to the left of the gate.

"That is right, is it not?"

Skip held out a hand, and raised a gun with the other.

"Is it not?"

"You're a little bold without your toy soldiers, aren't you?" quipped Carly.

As if on cue, a series of clicks and clacks signaled the loading and cocking of rifles, as Pandora Dawn in its entirety stepped out of the shadows behind Skip.

"I will take the key now."

"Okay," said Ridley.

He sunk his hand into his pocket and produced the ring.

Skip smiled to himself. "Of course. Kahlid's ring. Taken from him by the Emir. Now, toss it to me."

Ridley lifted the ring, but was stopped by the sound of whispers again. He glanced down the alley to his right and saw the figure once again, beckoning. Their path was clear.

"Run!" Ridley shouted to Carly.

Together they took off down the alley, sprinting and kicking up sand as they went.

"Go! Get them!" Skip shouted, and he and his soldiers followed after.

Ridley and Carly were a hundred feet down the alley already.

"Who's that?" she asked, gesturing toward the figure.

"Oh. Good. You can see them too."

They didn't have time to discuss or react, much less take in the impressive colonnade that extended before them on either side. There was a rumbling behind them.

Ridley glanced back to see Pandora Dawn not far behind. Skip was moving at a rather surprising clip, dogging their steps. But, what caught Ridley's eye was the guardians. They were already on their feet and moving faster. They moved down the colonnade, crushing men with every step. Some of them fired their rifles impotently, only to be swept up by giant stone hands and flung into the air, or smashed against the architecture.

The guardians were almost on them. Another thirty feet and they would be just as dead as the others. Why hadn't it worked? He was so sure. But, now....

Ridley hit the sand hard with someone on top of him. They swung and hit him repeatedly. Ridley scrambled to throw them off. All around him he could hear the sounds of gunfire and screams, and the heavy stone footfalls. A large shadow loomed over him.

Suddenly, it stopped. All of it. The sounds. The hits. It was silent again. Ridley rolled over. First he saw Carly, stock still and staring upward. Next he saw the Pandora Dawn mercs. They were all the same. Still and staring. On top of him was Skip, frozen and looking up like the others. Beyond them all, the guardians were frozen, looming over them.

The wind whistled by.

"Uhhh. What do we do?" asked one of the mercs.

"Shut up, Mike!" said another.

The guardians slowly turned and walked back down the alley, retaking their places to either side.

"Well," said Skip, as he climbed off Ridley. "Looks like we will be sticking quite close together."

Once he was on his feet, he pulled an old Webley pistol and trained it on Ridley. "Up you get. Go on."

Carly helped Ridley up as the remaining mercenaries moved in, guns brandished.

For the first time, the whole party was able to get a good look at the city. From its exterior–though glistening white–it had not been wholly remarkable in its design, and the way the shined walls had caught the light kept anyone from looking directly at it until close enough that the exterior walls blocked their view.

Inside the city there were massive buildings of marble. Columns and archways.

"Remarkable," said Skip, "The architecture. It is a composite. I see Italian, English, French, and Hungarian. All of which harmoniously united by an overall Byzantine discipline."

"The Crusaders," said Carly.

"I guess the legend was right," Ridley broke in. "They must have gotten lost on their way back to Europe."

"But where are all the people now?" Carly asked.

The group went quiet, listening. There was a howl of wind. And something else.

"Do you guys hear that?" asked Mike.

"Shut up, Mike!"

"You shut up, Howard!"

"Crack team you've got there, Skip," quipped Carly.

"No, I'm serious," said Mike. "Listen."

They all listened closely.

"I hear it," said Ridley. "Sounds like...water. This way."

Ridley started to walk toward the sound, but stopped suddenly at the sound of Skip pulling back the hammer of his gun.

"Carry on," Skip said. "I just advise you not to stray too far."

The group walked on through the eerily silent streets of the city. The surviving seven Pandora Dawn mercenaries instinctively checked their corners for tangos they knew wouldn't be there. It was normalcy for them. The only sanity they had left to cling to in this empty city.

"This plan of yours," asked Carly, leaning close. "What happened next?"

Ridley shrugged.

"Honestly, I was expecting the statues to kill them. The rest of this? I'm just making this up as I go."

"Great," said Carly, rolling her eyes before taking stock

of her resources and circumstances.

"Weren't there supposed to be piles of gold or something?" one of the mercenaries asked.

"There better be," another muttered under his breath.

"Just up ahead," said Ridley, with feigned confidence.

They turned a corner and stepped out into a large square. The sun was beginning to rise over the city and the variously-colored marble seemed to glow all around them. The center of the square was sunken and tiered. At its center a gargantuan fountain still flowed. It looked to have once been a bathing pool. Around its edges, at the various levels, were merchant booths where street hawkers had once stalled their wares. Once, but not for some time.

"My God," said Ridley.

"Look at them all," Carly said, her hand at her mouth.

They weren't looking at the booths, or the fountain, or even the glowing marble. It was the bodies. They were everywhere. Littering the ground. Doubled over the booths. Piled high against the walls of buildings, and spilling out of the windows. They were old. Little more than skeletons at this point. But, by all appearances, they looked to have died screaming.

Their jaws were locked open. Dried, leather tendrils of remaining flesh stretched tight over the cheeks. All of them were like this. Their silent screams unending. Still in time.

"There must be thousands of them," said Carly.

"Why the hell are they all here?" asked Ridley "We didn't see a single one anywhere else in the city."

"I don't like this," said Mike.

"Stop your whining," said Skip, turning. "You think I give a damn what you like?"

He raised his pistol, but stopped. Something had caught his eye.

The whispering caught the rest of the group's attention and they all turned to see that the figure had returned. The mercs' muscle memories brought their rifles to the ready and they struck battle stances, ready to light it up at a word. The figure didn't move. Nor did Ridley or Carly. Only Skip took a few halting steps forward, awestruck.

"Lower your weapons," he told his men.

"But, Sir—"

"Drop them!"

The men did as they were told, letting the shoulder

straps take their loads.

"There is nothing to fear here," said Skip, still slowly approaching the being.

Something had happened to him. At the sight of it, he had softened. The steely man was gone. This was a man of pure wonderment. Perhaps a faint glimmer of who he had been when first leaving to explore the world outside his little fishing village. Maybe this was Nick's Skip.

The figure continued unmoved. It called to them. Not in a voice, as such. Rather, something about it asked them to follow, and they did. One by one, their feet stirred, lifting from the sandy stone streets, and padding forward. The figure turned slowly, and lead on.

-

"Do you hear that?" asked Carly.

"That clicking, popping sound? Like giant rice krispies?" asked Ridley. "Yeah."

"It's been going since we left the square."

"Hardly the strangest part of our day."

He was right. They had been following the figure, its samite gowns still flowing in unfelt winds, for roughly twenty minutes. In that time they had passed through temples, and noble homes that were draped in fine tapestries and gilded furniture. Copper, silver, and gold. Jewels and pearls. All of which were freely left about. Forgotten or rejected by their owners in whatever had driven them from their homes.

The mercenaries, of course, glanced around as they moved through. Perhaps making mental notes for their return trip. But, none of them ever stopped moving. Never stopped walking. Whatever it was about the figure that had stirred them to movement in the first place had not yet weakened. Driving them onward near hypnotically. But, even so, the eyes of greedy men are apt to wander.

Skip seemed not to notice. The treasures, or the temples, or the noble homes. He hadn't said a word since their trek began. The figure's most dutiful follower.

The sound. The cracking, popping sound, was growing closer. Louder.

-

Their path lead them deep into the center of the city, towards what could only be a palace. A gargantuan building sat atop a large stone platform, like a ziggurat, with intimidating stairs to climb. The gain was easily a thousand feet, and as they began, Ridley cursed his long-abandoned exercise regimen, not to mention his recently suffered injuries.

His muscles strained to lift him up the steep steps, and as they got higher, the wind picked up, threatening to pull them all from the palace's side and toss them to the empty streets below. No. Not empty.

From this vantage, Ridley could see that the streets weren't empty. Down below, people were milling around in the streets. Carrying on with their days as if it was any other. He gestured for Carly's attention and pointed. She looked, before turning back to him. Her face wasn't one of confusion. It was of concern. It bordered on fear.

They reached the top. Skip, Carly, and the mercenaries seemed unfazed by the climb. Ridley, however, came over the edge on all fours. Breathing heavily and cursing them all.

"You okay?" Carly asked.

"That's a relative question, no?"

She smiled at him before helping him to his feet.

They had expected a palace, and what stood before them was a palace, but not as they might have imagined.

The top of the platform was crowned with a circular cloister. Vines draped over and clung to the stone columns, surrounding a pool. In and around the pool, noble men and women laughed and played in the nude. Splashing one another with water, and feasting on the sumptuous food that was laid out by servants. At the center, just beyond the large pool, sat a man and woman on large golden thrones.

"What the fuck?" asked Mike. A servant brushed passed him carrying a tray piled high with various fruits, and made for the table.

"I don't think they see us," said Ridley, waving his hand in front of one of the nude nobles, and receiving no reaction.

Skip had walked to the edge of the pool and stopped. The figure strode across the pool's surface and without a moment's hesitation sat in the queen's chair, merging with the woman who sat there.

"What have you brought us?" the queen asked.

The group looked from one to another in confusion.

Skip, feeling emboldened, opened his mouth to speak. "Your Highness, I–"

"Only the finest, my queen," another voice cut in.

They all turned to see a very proud looking noble man. He was covered head to toe in heavy-looking white vestments, and smiled as he lead a group toward the throne. They were ten scared-looking young women with their hands tied, and to either side of them tall men in armor.

"Approach," said the queen.

The noble bowed and made his long way around the pool to kneel by the queen's feet. The king all the while seemed uninterested, instead languidly switching between his wine and a hookah.

When the queen had given the sign for him to stand, the noble did such and turned to look at the girls. Waving over them in a dramatic gesture, his hands, for the first time, became clear. A ring graced his hand. Gold with a large ruby.

"I think that's Hamid," said Ridley to Carly before realizing she wasn't still beside him.

"These girls," continued Hamid, "were found on the route from Benghazi."

"Not alone, were they?" asked the queen.

"No, my queen. They were minded, but your men made short work of them."

281

Hamid continued to talk and expound on the way in which they had so honorably kidnapped these poor girls.

Ridley looked around for Carly and found her at the platform's edge, looking down on the city. He went to approach her, but something, instead, caught his eye. One of the girls was clearly sick. No. Not one. Several of them. Their eyes were bloodshot, skin pale, and sweat flowed freely over their brows. More than the climb would have induced.

The queen gestured, and the soldiers forced the girls to the pool's edge. The nude, prancing nobles had not ceased their revelry. Clearly slave trading was not at all unusual to them, let alone a reason to stop enjoying themselves.

Skip and his men were transfixed by whatever it was they were seeing. Were they ghosts? Was this some sort of time loop?

Ridley turned away from it all and went to Carly, who was still standing with her back to them, looking down on the city.

"What is it?" he asked her.

She turned to him slowly.

"You don't see it?"

He held her gaze for a moment. Her eyes were

panicked. Of all of the faces he had seen her wear, he had never seen this. This was something else. True, genuine terror.

He looked down and out at the city. Immediately he saw two things. On the highest crown of every building, all across the city, domes, towers, and cupolas, a single word was written in giant, jagged, red letters:

JINN

In the hazy recesses of Ridley's esoteric knowledge, the word found meaning. It was an Arabic word in English. It had one meaning. Evil Spirits. The angry dead. And that was what he saw next.

All the people who had suddenly appeared in the streets were no longer milling about in their daily duties. They were heading for the platform. Scaling it. Climbing and crushing one another. As they got close enough for him to make them out, he saw that they weren't people. No. Not anymore. These were the skeletons they had seen earlier. Or rather, they were among them. As he quickly glanced around he saw that there were several squares like the one they had seen. All of them with fountains, and all of them the source of these newly animated horrors. Their bones cracking and popping.

Ridley slowly backed away from the edge. A scream rang out, and he spun to see one of the captured girls face down

283

in the pool. Soon after, another collapsed, and another, and so on. It was the nude revelers that were screaming. Unsure how to react. Something dark spread from the girls' bodies, weaving through the waters and taking hold of revelers. Taking hold, and taking control. Chaos broke out.

"What the hell?! What the hell?!" The mercenaries were panicking.

Mike backed away, his rifle raised.

"God damnit! Lower your rifle, man!" shouted Skip. "They are not real. None of this is."

Mike wouldn't listen. Maybe he couldn't. The fear was so totally in control that it had filtered out any argument against getting out. Getting away. He took another step back, and that was when the skeletal arm, with its fine garments and long-vanished flesh, reached up and grabbed him. Mike whipped around, screamed, and managed to fire a few shots before all the many other arms reached up to pull him down. He let out a terrified shriek before switching to full auto and letting them have it.

"What do we do? Ridley, what do we do?!" Carly was losing it. Ridley was barely holding on himself, but whatever he had he needed to keep for her sake.

The skeletons were crowding and pouring over the

edges on to the platform, as Ridley took hold of Carly's hand and guided her towards the mercenaries. Skip pulled a side arm from one of his men and took aim.

"Put the bastards down," said Skip.

On that order, the remaining men of Pandora Dawn unleashed hell. A storm of bullets shredded the skeletons, turning pieces to powder. They fell, and were crushed by the next wave. There were bullets for those, too. Wave after wave came, and wave after wave went down. But, eventually the bullets began to run low.

"Sir, none of this will mean anything if we can't get off this thing," said one of the few mercenaries to maintain composure.

Skip nodded, still firing.

"If you have any ideas," he shouted to Ridley, "I am happy to hear them."

Ridley scanned around. What did they have? What were their options? There!

The queen's unshakeable decorum decayed to mad laughter, while the perpetually uninterested king had his throat torn out in a ragged mass, clenched in the teeth of a nude man.

But, just beyond them, Ridley saw what he needed. Hamid panicking at the unfolding chaos of naked cannibalism.

"Him! We need to follow him!"

"What?" asked Skip.

Ridley caught sight of a skeleton behind the old man. He pulled a sidearm from one of the mercenaries and, in one fluid motion, Bang!

"He escaped. We need to follow him."

Skip's lips curled into a smirk.

"You heard him, boys. After the Arab!"

As if on cue, Hamid overcame his panic just enough to run, ducking behind the two thrones and heading for a narrow stone stairway.

Ridley looked to Carly, who nodded and grabbed a handgun from the merc beside her.

"Let's go," she was back.

Ridley led the crowd in a full sprint around the edge of the pool, popping off shots left and right. The mercenaries were on point, but more of his missed than hit. Apparently it is far more difficult to hit a moving target if you're moving and terrified.

As the skeletons drew nearer, it took every fiber of discipline and sanity to stay on target and not lose sight of Hamid. Screams rang out behind, and Ridley glanced back just long enough to see the amassing horde behind them, as they overtook the two mercenaries covering the retreat.

When he whipped back around he was face-to-face with one of the boney horrors. He fell on his back, as it gnashed and gargled in front of him. Bits of dried flesh snapped as they stretched in unfamiliar movement. He could smell it.

BANG!

Its head exploded into shards.

Carly held out a hand. "Let's go."

They were up and over, heading down the stone stairway. It was narrow and extended over an arch to a lower building. Hamid was already making his way through the rooftop garden and toward another arched walkway.

There were no railings on the stairs–nor was there time for caution–and more than a few mercenaries fell. Either from the loss of balance, or the little bit of the horde that managed to maneuver the stairs. The vast majority of it poured over the edge like a sickening waterfall of bone and dust.

Ridley held his arms out to either side, maintaining his

balance, and with a quick sigh of relief touched down in the rooftop garden. No time to rest. Hamid was disappearing down that other walkway. How was he so fast?

The garden was thick with tropical plants, and mixed in among them were the dead whom the vines had grown through and reclaimed. Even they reached out and snapped as the group passed by. Others were half submerged in fountains and gurgled, limply attempting to do their hell spawn duty.

As they reached the next stairway, Hamid was just setting foot on the ground and heading for a manhole cover.

"Son of a bitch," said Ridley.

"Do you have a better idea?" asked Carly.

"No," Ridley replied in the nearest thing to a sulk he could manage given the circumstances.

Chapter 20

It had taken him the better part of the early morning, but Philippe had finally managed to muscle through the excruciating pain of his mostly scorched body and drag himself (a few times literally) from the medical tent, across the camp, and to the makeshift airstrip Pandora Dawn had prepared. He started that process just after the rest of them had left, and now that he managed to raise himself to a standing position at his destination, the sun had crested the dunes. At a guess, he figured it was maybe eight o'clock.

There were three large cargo planes, emblazoned with Pandora Dawn's branding. Their landing gear had, smartly, been modified with skids that would work on the shifting sands where standard tires would have just sank, unable to find purchase. He still wasn't certain they could get up to speed, though, as this sand was like fresh snow. Soft and powdery.

291

And for as long as the planes had been sitting, even the skids had begun to sink anyway.

As the sun climbed, the temperature rapidly followed suit, and as he began sweat, it ran into his wounds and stung fiercely. His vision went white. It burned and seared, and in an instant he was back in the flames. He remembered the impact as the plane had slammed into the sand. It had seemed much less soft back then. He remembered seeing the fuel leak and the spark that ignited. He remembered what it felt like to cook and to smell himself cooking.

He nearly lost his footing and snapped back in time to catch himself. Bracing on the door of one of the paramilitary group's trucks, he popped another of the painkillers he had snagged from the medical tent before setting out. Once his vision cleared again, he looked around at what he had on offer. A few Jeeps, a cargo truck, random cables, and whatever he could pull from the tents.

"C'est l'heure d'aller travailler," he said. Time to go to work.

He did.

-

Mike and another Pandora Dawn merc took point, cracking and dropping glow sticks down the manhole before following after them, rappelling on quickly-tied ropes. They hit the tunnel's floor with guns at the ready and, after a moment, signaled for the rest to follow them.

The rest of the mercs clipped on with carabineers and one by one dropped down into the tunnel. Their pursuers weren't on them yet, but it seemed to be only a matter of time. When it came to Skip, Ridley, and Carly, both men opted to send her first.

"When this is over," Skip said to Ridley, once she was out of earshot. "we should talk about your future."

He smiled while clipping his own carabineer to the rope. "Resilience like yours. That cannot be taught."

The old man hopped and slid down the rope and into the tunnel. For a brief moment, Ridley was alone with the cracking/popping sound and his thoughts. Unsure of which he preferred, he slid after the rest them.

When he landed, the mercs had already struck their battle stances and an order of procession.

"Which way now?" asked Carly.

"Listen," said Ridley.

They all fell silent. To their right, faint and in the distance, were the sounds of heavy breaths. But, before they could react, something else could be heard. To their left, much closer, was the cracking/popping.

"Go!" shouted Skip.

They ran through the tunnel, their flashlight beams dancing, and came to a T-junction. Ridley just caught sight of Hamid disappearing around a corner, and directed the rest to follow. The cracking/popping was getting closer. It was on all sides.

A scream rang out and when Ridley glanced back he saw a skeleton drop from the ceiling of the tunnel, landing on the mercenary bringing up the rear. It tore at him. Its snapping jaws bit hard into his throat and pulled away with a wet mass, decisively ending his screams.

Before any further reaction could be had, more of the skeletons poured out of the dark, ringing the tunnel. They clung to the walls and ceiling. Their progress just as horrifically fast, regardless of their surface.

The mercs unloaded on them, firing wildly in retreat. Ridley and Carly just ran. They didn't want to risk losing sight of Hamid. He was their only lifeline. They had descended into hell and were chasing a ghost. But, what more could they do? Skip was behind them. Mike was just beyond. And past him, there was only a mingled mass of gunfire and screams. The ratio began to tip and soon the gunfire was the minority. Then it was gone. The screams followed.

There was light ahead. They rounded another corner and found that the light was pouring from the ceiling. An open manhole cover. There were a couple of stone blocks stacked just below it. Clearly how Hamid had escaped.

"Go! Up!" Ridley shouted to Carly.

She didn't need to be told. And in an instant she was up the blacks and leaped, grabbing hold of the manhole's edge and lifting herself. Once she was through, she turned back and extended an arm to Ridley, whose upper body strength was comparatively lacking. He was up and through.

They were back near the gate. The streets around them were still clear. The only skeletons here were inert, still cast about in their final poses of a painful death. Instinctively, Ridley looked back into the hole, and saw that Mike was climbing up after them.

"Please!" he shouted. "Please don't leave me here!"

He leapt and Ridley reached for him, but before their hands met, he was grabbed and swept away screaming by a wave of the Jinn. Ridley and Carly could hear his screams grow progressively quieter and more distant as he was carried deep into the city's tunnels. For what purpose, they were better off not guessing.

A few more gunshots rang out, and Ridley looked again to see Skip step into the beam of light, still firing on the Jinn. He turned to climb, but there was a problem. That last group had toppled Kahlid's stack of stones when they took Mike. There was nothing to climb on. No time to re-stack them. Skip simply looked up at Ridley, and smiled.

"Let's go," said Carly, and they did.

As they stepped away, a final gunshot rang out.

Their attention returned to the gate, and they strode into the colonnade with cautious confidence. This part, at least, they knew how to deal with. They made it about forty feet before the rumbling started.

"Oh, what the fuck?!" shouted Ridley.

A sinking feeling hit the pit of his stomach when he checked his pocket. The ring was gone. As the guardians of the gate stood, preparing to do their duties, Carly glanced back to see the Jinn emerging from the manhole, and from the alleyways and streets behind them. She and Ridley looked to each other. He grabbed her hard around the waist, pulling her close, and kissed her with the power and passion of a dying man's last kiss.

"Run," he said.

The two of them bolted for the exit as the Jinn poured into the colonnade behind them, and the guardians stepped over the gate's arch and into their path. They didn't break pace or stride. Full speed. Straight on till dawn. Their arms pumped furiously, slicing the air in front of them.

They were fifty feet from the guardians now, and the Jinn were close enough behind for them to hear the snapping of tendons. The guardian to the left leaned low, sliding its left hand along the ground like a spatula, while the one on the right readied itself to smack whatever the first flipped up out of the air. Neither of them broke pace. The massive obsidian hand slid closer and closer.

At the last moment, Ridley let go of Carly's hand and shoved her to the left as he dove right. The hand passed between them and scooped up a large number of the Jinn before tossing them into the air where the other followed through. As the second hand met the airborne skeletons, they exploded into bone dust and fragments that rained down over them.

"Go! Go!" Ridley shouted to the still-dazed Carly.

They both climbed to their feet and continued running, weaving between the guardian's massive stone feet. The guardians themselves seemed unclear how to react, and quickly tried to turn around in the narrow colonnade as the Jinn washed over their feet and legs. For a moment, they seemed to do an awkward bit of dancing before one tripped into the other.

With a colossal bang, the statues slammed together and cracked, beginning to crumble. Their momentum kept them moving toward the gate, and the huge pieces of stone that once resembled men tumbled down, crushing everything in the colonnade, and even bits of the colonnade itself. Ridley and Carly dodged and ducked, but there was no escaping the thought that this was how it might end.

They were so close to the end, and the remaining Jinn were even closer behind them. Ridley put on a final burst of speed and sprinted, his muscles screaming. He leapt and landed hard in the sand as the final large piece of statue head landed exactly where the gate had stood. He had made it out.

He lay there panting for a while, staring into the massive eye that looked back at him. From under it and a few places to either side, he could see skeletal arms still desperately trying to scratch and claw their ways free from the rubble. But, it was over. He wondered idly how long it might take for them to realize it, or if they ever would. Would they scratch like that forever? Or at least until the bones wore down to nothing?

A cough came from his right, and Ridley's adrenaline-delirious mind suddenly remembered Carly. He looked over to see her lying on her back, not far from where he himself had landed. He crawled over to her.

"Are you okay?" he asked, aware of how silly a question it sounded.

"Do me a favor?" she asked.

"Anything," he said without hesitation.

"Next time I'm in Tangier, remind me not to go home with the rogue adventurer."

"Agreed," Ridley said with a smile. He climbed to his feet and extended a hand to help her up. She took it.

"Oh. And by the way. Shove me like that again, and I'll break your legs."

He thought on this for a moment before offering, "Fair enough."

"Love you," she said, sweetly.

"Love you, too."

When Ridley and Carly finally made it back to the camp, they found the medical tent empty.

"Where the hell did he go?" Ridley asked.

As if on cue, the sound of a truck engine trying and failing to turn over carried in through the canvas flap window.

They followed the sound and found Philippe standing, half-bent over the engine of a truck. As they approached, Ridley noticed that the truck's trailer hitch bore a cable that extended down and around the front landing gear of a large cargo plane, before meeting its other end at the hitch of another truck parked parallel to the first.

"You've been busy," said Carly.

Philippe shot quickly upright, startled by their approach, and nailed the back of his head on the truck's hood.

"Mon Dieu!" he shouted, while holding a hand to the spot that would soon be a bump.

He looked at the two of them appraisingly. "You're alive."

"Yeah. Well, you should see the other guys," said

Ridley, gesturing back toward the city.

Philippe followed his gesture and saw the pile of wreckage and bones that had been the city's gate. He seemed unsurprised.

"I saw," he said. "Decided I was better off over here."

"That's probably true," said Carly. "You want to tell us what you're working on?"

She pointed down to the snaking cable.

Philippe wiped the grease from his hands and grabbed the crutch he hadn't thought to grab from the med tent until about an hour previous. He moved along the cable, and the two followed them.

"The problem," he said, "is that this plane is too fucking heavy for the sand. The bastards were smart enough to skid the wheels, but we'll need to pull them free before we can even try to get her up to speed."

"So, she and I drive the trucks, tow the thing free, lamb back, and climb onboard before you leave us here," said Ridley.

"Oui."

Carly laughed while walking over to one of the trucks. "Guess it's a good thing we made it out, or you'd be stuck here."

As she finished speaking, she turned and climbed up to the cab and saw that the steering wheel of the truck had been tied with cables to keep it on a straight course.

"Oh," she said. "You were totally planning for us not to come back."

Philippe just shrugged. "Oui."

Suddenly, he froze.

"Philippe? What's up?" asked Ridley.

In answer, Philippe just pointed. They both followed his gesture and froze just the same. A wall of sand and wind was heading in their direction. Miles away, but approaching all the same. They had maybe a half hour before it would sweep over them.

-

"Okay. Let's do this," Ridley said with feigned confidence, as he turned the ignition of his truck. Carly did the same, and once both of them were running, they gave Philippe a thumbs up. With that, he started up the plane's engines.

Carly held up a three count, and once all her fingers were down, they dropped their trucks into gear and started rolling forward. They moved slowly at first, allowing the cable slack to gather up and go taut. But, the weight of the plane fought them and they had to start gunning. The truck wheels started to spin, and soon they were sinking, too.

Philippe pushed the throttle on the plane, and while it fought him as well, it couldn't fight physics. It slid forward, just a bit. Just enough for the cable to go a bit slack. That was enough for the trucks to catch again and move forward just slightly. They kept this up for a while. Long enough that the truck's engines threatened to redline. The cable around the landing gear was pulled so tight, that were it to snap at this point, it could cut through the truck like nothing.

Ridley looked to Carly. She was on task. Double clutching and shifting for every bit of traction she could get. As he turned back to his own work, something caught his eye. Something in the side view mirror. Movement. Maybe a shadow. He ran his hand over his eyes to wipe sweat away, and looked again. Nothing but the rapidly encroaching sand storm.

The wheels finally pulled free and they were in motion. The three of them steered for a distant dune and aimed dead on. Ridley and Carly both quickly set to lashing their respective steering wheels in place, before wedging the accelerators down with discarded rifles. They bailed out and ran, dodging the cargo plane's massive propellers, and met at the open rear cargo gate.

Once on board, Ridley walked over and grabbed the mic for the plane's intercom.

"We're all aboard and good to go," he said. "Close her up."

Carly gave him a big kiss and headed off for the cockpit. He watched her as she walked off, a smile unconsciously creeping to his face. They'd done it. All of it. They were done.

He didn't hear the gunshot. He only felt the force.

The bullet entered through his back and tore out through the front, passing through the meaty part of his right love handle. Ridley dropped to his knees as Carly turned to see Skip standing on the cargo ramp. His pistol was still smoking as he stepped forward into the plane proper.

He was torn up pretty bad. His clothes were ripped and bloody. A portion of his scalp hung loosely like a flap, held in place by the torn piece of shirt he had tied around his head to cover his missing right eye. The pistol was trained on Carly, and he moved slowly toward her. A man in complete control of

the situation.

"Hello, Darling," he said seductively. "Now, I hope you were not thinking of leaving without me." As he spoke, he walked over and pressed the large red button that closed the cargo ramp.

In the cockpit, Philippe watched as the two trucks neared the edge of the dune, and pulled up just as they dropped over the edge. The speed was just this side of right, and though it dipped a bit, he was able to get her in the air. As the sand rapidly dropped from under them, he quickly made to get them as far away as possible from the sand that was rapidly heading for them. He swung the plane around, positioning the storm at their tail.

Ridley lay on the floor clutching his gut, and Skip stepped over him, still fixing his gun on Carly.

"I must say. It was not very kind of you to just walk away like that. I will, of course, leave out the part where you tried to steal my plane as that is just bad manners."

Carly looked around. There was a rack of rifles off to her left, but they were too far and she had no cover between them. She was stuck.

"How'd you get out?" she asked.

"Honestly, it was not that hard. Though clearly, I did not make it unscathed. The two of you made quite the distraction. I suppose your egress would have been a bit easier had you still had this." With that he held up the ring that had vanished from Ridley's pocket.

"Forgive me," he said. "Old habits and sticky fingers. I was hoping to avoid the two of you sneaking away. Lot of good that did."

Skip paused for a moment. He pulled a flask from his pocket and took a long drink from it, turning its bottom skyward. Once it was empty, he tossed it aside, and Carly could swear that he looked, somehow, younger. He seemed stronger and his wounds seemed less ragged.

"I suppose you have your Frenchman at the stick. I must say, I am impressed by his resilience. Burns like those he–"

Before he could finish his thought, Ridley was up and clocked him across the face. The gun was out of his hand and slid across the floor. Carly dove for it.

"That was a mistake," Skip said, wiping blood from his mouth. He charged Ridley and the two of them slammed into the wall where Skip proceeded to pound him in the gut, giving extra attention to his gunshot wound. Ridley's vision went blinding white with pain, and he swung wildly. The old military man countered it and threw him across the cargo hold.

"Don't you fucking move!" shouted Carly.

Skip looked at her for a moment, then disregarded her and went back to beating the tar out of Ridley. She pulled the trigger. Nothing happened.

"Sorry about that, Darling," Skip said between punches. "Spent the rest of them on those damn Jinn. Which is fine by me. I'll just have to kill you all the old fashioned way."

Carly dropped the pistol and ran for the rifle rack. It was locked.

"Fuck!"

Ridley caught a lucky break and managed to nail Skip in the chest with a kick. The old man fell back, and Ridley climbed shakily to his feet.

"Okay, you son of a bitch," Ridley said. "In the past month I have lost my best friend, been chased more times than I can count, shot at, nearly crushed by statues, ripped apart by fucking skeletons, and then actually shot. And you know what really pisses me off? All I wanted to do was smoke weed and write. But, here we are!"

"Here we are," smiled Skip.

Ridley beckoned him. Skip came at him fast, but this time he was ready. He dodged the punch, brushing it aside with   307 his right while punching him square in the gut with his left. While he was stunned and breathless, Ridley grabbed a hold of his belt, and quickly spun and tossed him so he landed hard on his back.

Skip just laughed. It was a pained laugh, garbled by the mix of blood and mucus in his throat, and came out sounding all the more evil for it.

"The boy has some fight in him after all," he choked out through blood-stained teeth. And, before either of them could react, he was back up and charging on Ridley, slamming him hard against the wall and hitting the red button for the ramp.

They were high enough now–and the sand storm near enough–that wind rushed in at them, buffeted them around, and threatened to pull them back out.

Carly jumped and grabbed hold of a ratchet strap that lay slack on the floor. As the wind pulled at the three of them and she slid for the opening gate, she hooked the strap into a floor-mounted securing loop. As she ran out of slack she stopped with a hard shock and dangled, in mid-air, just inside the gate. The storm roared like some unholy beast, its jaws just beyond the plane's tail.

She looked back to see Ridley and Skip both clinging to a cargo net and continuing to exchange blows.

Skip punched Ridley square in the face, and it dazed him enough that he let go of the net and fell, just barely catching hold of the end.

"You know," Skip said, climbing down the net toward Ridley. "I never had any real quarrel with Ponsley. That was Burns. I always found him charming and a good laugh. But, if you represent the company he came to keep, I must say, he went soft in his old age."

With that he kicked for Ridley, and missed. Ridley grabbed him by the ankle instead and pulled hard, breaking Skip's grip on the net. The old man grabbed frantically, seeming to lose his reserve for the first time. He caught himself again and he and Ridley were eye to eye.

"He was my friend," said Ridley. "His name was Nick."

Ridley wound up and nailed Skip with a hard jab to the nose. The old man lost his grip and fell. The rush of wind ripped at him, and all Carly could do was swing out of his path. Together, she and Ridley watched as Skip James was swallowed by the storm. He disappeared into the swirling sand, and was gone.

"Ridley!" Carly shouted.

He broke his gaze at the storm and looked back to Carly. She pointed to the gate control and, after carefully navigating the still flapping cargo net, he was able to reach it and close the storm out. Without the wind to keep them aloft, they both hit the ground hard.

Painfully, they stood and came together. They held one another close and, for a long while, said nothing. It was over. This time, it was actually over.

They made their way to the cockpit and took their seats alongside Philippe.

"What happened to you?" he asked when he saw Ridley's condition.

"Some unfinished business. What do we do about the storm?" Ridley asked

But by the time he spoke, the winds had already begun to die down. The storm was tamed, and the sand it carried fell softly like a late winter snow. The desert had claimed its own.

Chapter 21

"Is Professor Gutwein in? We have an appointment," said Carly to the desk attendant at the British Museum.

"Your name?" asked the young woman.

"Carly Deloro."

"Just a moment."

She picked up a phone and dialed, and as she did so, Carly turned to Ridley, who sat on a low leather-cushioned bench by the door.

"You sure about this?" she asked.

He cracked a broad smile. "I'll get you another one. I promise."

"Miss Deloro?" asked a voice behind them, and they

both turned to see a funny little man in a tweed blazer. He was younger than they both expected, but the name tag on his front pocket read PAUL GUTWEIN.

He extended a hand and Carly took it.

"Yes. Hello professor," she said.

"Well, let's see what you have.

-

Neon lights flicked on and magnifying glasses on metal arms were swung into place around a small pedestal. From her pocket, Carly produced a small velvet bag, which she handed to the professor. He accepted it as if she had just trusted him with a newborn child and, after putting on gloves and picking up a large rubber tipped pair of tweezers, opened the bag and removed its contents.

The ring seemed somehow dull under the neon, but the stone still held a fire to it, even if it was an ember to the blaze it held in the desert.

"My God," said the professor. He placed it on the pedestal and adjusted his various lights and viewing equipment.

"Clearly of northern European craftsmanship. Late…thirteenth century, if I were to hazard a guess. Where did you say you got it?"

"It was a gift," said Ridley. "From an old friend."

-

Ridley eased his still-sore body into a seat on the Central Line tube, doing his best not to pop the stitches of his gunshot wound.

"You okay?" Carly asked as she crouched in front of him.

"That's relatively speaking, right?" he smirked back through the pain.

Carly's hand went to her bag, where she pulled out an unlabeled bottle of pills, extracted two, and handed them to him along with a bottle of water.

"We'll be back to the airstrip in a little over an hour. You can sleep on the plane," she said.

Ridley downed the pills and gulped the water.

"Where do we go next?"

Carly shrugged. "World's our oyster, right?"

He smiled at her, amazed and thankful for her very existence. All they had seen, all they had done, and here she was. She was all he needed and, inexplicably to him, he was the same to her.

"How would you like to meet my family?" he asked.

She turned and sat beside him, letting out a low whistle.

"Now, there's an adventure," she said.

The train rattled off with the two of them, and Ridley knew he had done what Nick never had. He found the life of adventure. But, he wouldn't live it alone.

A native of New Jersey, A.E. Fletcher currently resides in Los Angeles with a dachshund, continuing to write, and traveling whenever possible.